D0065320

In
Caverns
of
Blue
Ice

In Caverns of Blue Ice

A Novel by
Robert Roper

Sierra Club Books • San Francisco

Little, Brown and Company • Boston • Toronto • London

The Sierra Club, founded in 1892 by John Muir, has devoted itself to the study and protection of the earth's scenic and ecological resources — mountains, wetlands, woodlands, wild shores and rivers, deserts, and plains. The publishing program of the Sierra Club offers books to the public as a nonprofit educational service in the hope that they may enlarge the public's understanding of the club's basic concerns. The Sierra Club has some sixty chapters in the United States and in Canada. For information about how you may participate in its programs to preserve wilderness and the quality of life, please address inquiries to Sierra Club, 730 Polk Street, San Francisco, CA 94109.

First Edition

Library of Congress Cataloging-in-Publication Data

Roper, Robert, 1946–
In caverns of blue ice : a novel / by Robert Roper. — 1st ed.
p. cm.
Summary: A young mountaineer in love with another climber faces the ultimate test of her life in the blue ice of the Himalayas.
ISBN 0-316-75606-7
[1. Mountaineering — Fiction.] I. Title.
PZ7.R6789In 1991
[Fic] — dc20 90-27004

Sierra Club Books/Little, Brown children's books are published by Little, Brown and Company (Inc.) in association with Sierra Club Books.

10 9 8 7 6 5 4 3 2 1

HC

Published simultaneously in Canada by
Little, Brown & Company (Canada) Limited

Printed in the United States of America

This story is for my daughter,
Caitlin, who inspired it
and believed it, and
who fills a father's heart

Glossary of Mountaineering Terms

Arête	A well-defined ridge on a mountain, often with a sharp edge.
Belay	To protect a fellow climber by means of a rope tied to his body. The belayer, who holds the other end of the rope, saves the climber in the event of a fall.
Bergschrund	The place where the ice of a glacier meets a mountain wall. Often the ice melts away from the rock, creating a deep gap that climbers have a hard time getting across.
Bivouac	To sleep out on a mountain, often in very harsh conditions.
Chimney	A crack or tunnel up through the rock of a mountain, wide enough for a climber's body to fit inside.
Col	A high pass on a mountain ridge.

Couloir	A very steep gully worn in a mountain face by avalanches of snow and ice.
Crampons	Steel "teeth" that can be attached to a climber's boots, for moving over snow and ice.
Crevasse	A crack in the massive ice of a glacier; can be hundreds of feet deep.
Dièdre	Where two walls of rock come together at a right angle, as in the corner of a room.
Headwall	The massive, steep rock formation just below the summit of a great mountain.
Massif	A section of a mountain range, containing one or more summits.
Pitch	A section of a climb between two belay positions. The length of the section is often determined by the length of the climbing rope, about sixty yards.
Piton	A metal spike for hammering into cracks in a rock wall.
Rappel	To slide down a rope attached to a mountain face. Usually the rope hangs double from the point of attachment; thus, it can be retrieved from below by pulling on one end.
Traverse	To climb to either side on a mountain, rather than straight up or down.

In Caverns of Blue Ice

One

The little town of Montier, in southeastern France, sits in a narrow valley high in the mountains. All the houses are built of stone. The streets are paved with stones, the Catholic church is made of stone, the air itself smells of stone — the stone from the steep, treacherous cliffs rising up on every side.

As recently as seventy years ago, no real roads went to Montier. Travelers to that remote corner of the Alps had to hike many miles along narrow, rocky paths, with their belongings strapped to their backs. In the winter, the snow sometimes piles up to a depth of thirty feet. In spring and summer, the meadows nearby fill with a lush growth of grass, and sheep and cattle are let out to graze. The people of Montier, mostly shepherds and farmers in the old days, sometimes passed their entire lives without venturing out of their valley.

More than a hundred years ago, a stranger arrived in Montier. He was a rich man from Paris, and after looking up at the fearsome cliffs all around, he asked if anyone would help him climb them. At first, no one volunteered. The gentleman pulled a bag containing louis d'or out of his pocket, and the farmers of the town, who had never before seen so much money, became more interested. One of them said:

"The cliffs here are full of demons, monsieur — you're asking us to risk our lives. No one can climb these horrible mountains, no one. If God had meant us to climb the mountains, He would've given us feet like a goat's."

The gentleman calmly added five more coins to the pile in his hand. The farmers gasped, shaking their heads at the sight of so much wealth all in one place. But still, no one came forward.

"Are you cowards, then?" the gentleman asked quietly. "Do all of you believe in 'demons,' that sort of rubbish?"

"I'm not sure I do."

The voice came from the rear of the crowd. Everyone stepped back to have a look at the speaker. But it was only a young shepherd, fourteen or fifteen years old.

"Very well," the gentleman said, looking the boy up and down. "Then will you guide me to the base of the cliffs? And will you climb with me as far as we can go?"

The young shepherd said nothing. He looked up at the mountaintops, some of them covered with snow. No one from Montier had ever climbed the local cliffs — it was considered dangerous just to walk close to them. The Devil himself supposedly lived on one of the glaciers, in the shadow of a mountain shaped like a witch's nose.

"I'll tell you what," the boy finally said. "Take your bag of money and give it to the priest in town. If we don't come back, he can give it to the poor, to the needy. And if we do come back — well, then, I'll keep it for myself."

The gentleman and the shepherd set out early the next morning. No one knows which cliffs they climbed, but they returned a few days later, still alive. The name of the young shepherd was Auguste DeMaistre (later nicknamed "Red-beard"). One of his gold louis d'or, mounted in a glass case, can be seen even today in a certain rooming house in the town of Montier.

Louise DeMaistre was the great-granddaughter of this first mountain guide, the red-bearded Auguste. Her mother, Martine Alby, came from a village several valleys to the south, close to the Italian border. Martine raised four children (Louise was the youngest) and ran a rooming house as well. Many famous climbers stayed at the rooming house, and Louise got to know them when still a little girl.

Louise's father, Jules DeMaistre, was a famous climber in his own right. In 1928, he climbed the Aiguille Blanche (The White Needle) in the French Alps. This was the first time the Needle had been climbed successfully, and many people had died in previous attempts. As a result of this adventure, Jules became famous all over Europe, and people began asking him to lead them on expeditions.

Jules DeMaistre is probably best known for the first

ascent of the Mur de la Mort (Wall of Death) in 1931. A wealthy Swiss doctor, Henri Clarton, hired him to lead a party of five climbers up the notorious Death Wall. Jules agreed, but he warned the doctor that this attempt would demand the utmost in skill and endurance, and that their chances for success were slim, at best. Nevertheless, the doctor was eager to go, and the climb began on the morning of August 4, 1931, in clear weather. On August 6, when the party had reached a point a little less than halfway up, one of the climbers dislodged a huge boulder, which fell on top of the man climbing below. (Max von Bern, the climber killed that day, was twenty-two years old and a dental student in Geneva. His body was never found.) The party — upset and badly demoralized — stopped where it was, on a narrow ledge about eighteen hundred feet above the base of the mountain. Here they passed a cold, miserable night.

The next morning, DeMaistre asked Dr. Clarton and the other remaining climbers whether they wanted to continue. There was much debate, but they finally decided to go on. However, at three that afternoon, a storm blew in, a late-summer blizzard of the type often encountered in the Alps. Soon the mountain was completely covered in snow and ice. Climbing was impossible in these conditions, and the party prepared to bivouac once again.

The following morning, the storm continued. Dr. Clarton examined his fellow climbers and declared that they were all suffering from frostbite to one degree or another, and that if they stayed on the mountain much longer, they would surely die. But there seemed to be no way to escape — the rocks were glassy with ice, and the group had brought along none of the special equipment needed for climbing in such conditions. Jules DeMaistre, as the leader of the group, felt a responsibility to attempt some kind of rescue; he knew it was impossible to climb down, but he thought he might, by himself, make it up to the top of the Death Wall. Once up there, he could possibly climb down by an easier route to summon help, and some of the other climbers might then be saved.

Under dreadful conditions, with no rope to catch him in case he fell, he continued up the mountain. Somehow he made it, over the icy rocks and fields of snow, and reached the summit a little past nightfall. (This was the first time the Wall of Death had been climbed by anyone, in good conditions or bad. It was twelve years before anyone climbed it again.) At the top, DeMaistre luckily ran into another party of climbers, who had come up the mountain by another, easier route, and they tied all their ropes together and lowered them over the side. Jules slid down the ropes, reached his half-frozen companions, and one by one brought them up the mountain to safety.

This was Louise DeMaistre's father — there can be no doubt that his great skill, his rare courage, were inspirations to her. Years later, when she was a famous climber herself, she always asked his advice before embarking on dangerous expeditions, and she humbly insisted that he was the better climber — even though she climbed many mountains that he never attempted.

Two

Louise DeMaistre was first too small, and then she was too big. When she was born she weighed only two and a half pounds, and no one expected her to live. Since her mother became ill just after giving birth, her chances for survival were even worse, because her mother couldn't nurse her. She was given out to a wet nurse, a woman who takes care of infants and feeds them her own breast milk. But the wet nurse complained that Louise drank too much, using up the milk that should have gone to her other babies. Only because Louise's father paid her three times the normal amount did the nurse agree to keep feeding Louise.

The tiny, scrawny infant soon grew healthy, and then she grew plump. Then — extra plump. She had a remarkably strong appetite, and by the time she was four she was considered to be really rather fat. Her older brothers and sister called her *peau de beurre* (butter skin). She was a pretty girl, with dark hair and eyes, who was not especially interested in school. She preferred helping her mother in the rooming house (she especially liked helping in the kitchen — the best place for someone who likes to eat). Unlike her brothers, who both wanted to be mountain guides, Louise wasn't very excited about the out-of-doors. She went on hikes and a few climbs with her father, but like her older sister, Elise, she considered mountain climbing something that "only the men" did. If someone had told her that one day she would be one of the most famous climbers in Europe — as good as or better than many great male climbers — she would have laughed out loud.

When Louise was twelve years old, a tragedy changed the course of her life. Her oldest brother, Rifi, then nineteen, consented to lead a party of Englishmen on a hike into the mountains. Rifi was a very strong, tall young man, a promising mountain climber who was only a year away from becoming an official guide. He had been climbing with his father since the age of six, and everybody who saw them together said that Rifi was the very image of his father, just as brave and almost as skillful. However, on the hike with the Englishmen, he fell down a crevasse on the glacier named Les Trois Dents (The Three Teeth). Rifi's body was never found. The DeMaistre family went into mourning, and Jules made his three surviving children promise that they would never go into the mountains again. To lose one son was bad enough, but to lose someone else would have been impossible, unbearable.

This wasn't hard for Louise to accept, but for her other

brother, Jean-Claude, it was a torture. Jean-Claude also had been an avid mountain climber since age six, and he, too, dreamed of one day becoming an official guide. Jean-Claude observed his father's prohibition against climbing for six months, but after that he began sneaking away whenever he could to practice on the steep granite walls of the Massif de la Vaudroise (the area of the Alps close to their village). But a climber can't climb alone. He needs a partner, someone to hold the rope that protects him if he falls. Having no one else, Jean-Claude asked Louise if she would sneak away with him. She refused, of course.

"All right, then I'll climb without a rope," Jean-Claude said bitterly. "But if I don't come back, you'll know what happened. There was no one to catch me, and I fell."

"That's not fair," Louise answered calmly. "If I don't go, then I'm responsible if you get hurt. But if I do, I'm disobeying Father. I can't win either way."

"I'm not asking so much. Come with me tomorrow, that's all. We won't go far. And if Father finds out, I'll say I made you come."

The next day, against her better judgment, Louise went with her brother into the hills. Only four miles from the town of Montier was a cliff known as Chapeau d'Henri (Henry's Hat). Louise had climbed here before, with her father, but now everything was different. When your father is one of the world's best mountaineers, somehow you don't worry so much. You know that if anything goes wrong, he'll save you, as he's saved many other people. But a fourteen-year-old brother is less reassuring. Besides, the death of their older brother was still on their minds. Louise could tell that Jean-Claude was thinking of Rifi as they got ready to start up the cliff.

"We can still turn back," she said warningly. "Maybe it's better if we don't go today — it looks like it might start to snow."

"No, it's not going to snow. Now stay close behind me, Louise. I don't want you slowing me down."

Near the top of Henry's Hat, after about two hours of climbing, they came to a steep, slippery part of the wall. The rock seemed as if it had been polished, and there were very few knobs to grab hold of. Jean-Claude tried to climb it first. He was attached to his sister by a sturdy rope, so if either of them fell, the other would be able to catch him. But a few yards up the wall Jean-Claude called down:

"Watch out! I think I'm about to come off. The rock's too smooth here — I can't stay on."

Louise prepared to catch her brother, and sure enough, a few seconds later he slipped, and only the rope, which Louise had wrapped around a rock, kept him from tumbling down the mountain.

"I don't think we can make it," Jean-Claude said nervously. "Let's go over to the left a few yards. Maybe there's an easier way up."

"All right."

But when they had traversed to the left, they saw that the wall was equally smooth there. The rock was shiny and slick everywhere: it was like trying to climb a wall of glass. Only one area offered them any chance of getting to the top. There were a few hand- and footholds, just enough for an expert climber to get up.

"I can't believe we climbed this with Father. It's just too hard," Louise said.

"Maybe we've gotten off the main route. Maybe nobody's ever climbed this part of the mountain before."

Once again, Jean-Claude started up. He made slow, difficult progress. When he was about fifty feet above her, he called down to Louise:

"I can't go much farther. I'm tired, and there's nothing to hold on to. If I could only get up another twenty feet, I'd be over that big ledge, and then it gets easier."

Louise called back up: "Take your time, Jean-Claude. Rest, then try to push on. But be careful. I don't want you to fall here."

A few minutes later, Jean-Claude started up again. But he seemed to have lost his nerve. He only advanced about five feet. Then he pressed his body against the rock.

"I just can't do it. It's too hard, Louise. It takes all my strength just to hold on."

"All right, stay there. I'll come up."

Something had happened. Louise, seeing her brother in a bad spot, lost all awareness of her own danger; without really thinking, she began to climb. Though younger and less experienced than her brother, she soon reached his position. She made sure he was attached securely to the rocks with the rope. Then she continued up till she reached the ledge above him.

"You were right," she shouted down, "it's easy from here

on. Just come up the way I did. Take hold of that little knob that looks like half a doughnut. Once you get your foot on that, it's easy."

Following Louise's instructions, Jean-Claude climbed up to the ledge. From there it was a simple climb to the top of the mountain. They returned home just before dark, and though their clothes were dirty and scuffed, as happens when you go climbing, no one said anything — not their mother, who gave them a late supper, and not even their father, who had been wondering where they were.

Three

For a long while, Louise forgot about the incident with Jean-Claude. This was just as well, because her brother was upset about it — he wasn't used to being outclimbed (or outplayed or outfought) by his younger sister.

"You must have used some trick," he said. "I wasn't feeling well that day, and climbing tired me. I bet I had a fever that afternoon."

"Quite possibly," Louise answered; she saw no reason to make him feel even worse about it.

"When you climbed to that ledge, it was luck that you happened to put your foot in the right place," he continued. "If I'd tried again, I'd have made it, too."

"I'm sure you would."

In fact, it didn't seem important to Louise that she had "outclimbed" her older brother. Climbing wasn't a contest; it was an act of cooperation, something you did with a friend, the two of you supporting one another. If anyone was supposed to get "beaten" in climbing, it was the mountain. Not your partner.

"Anyway, I don't think we should go again for a while, Jean-Claude. Father was nice not to yell at us that time, but I can tell he's worried. He's still thinking about Rifi. He doesn't want us to make a life in the mountains."

"No, I know he doesn't."

That spring — the year was 1950 — Louise was twelve and a half years old. She began to grow (of course, she had been growing all along, but this was something different, the growth spurt that teenagers often have), and by her birthday in September, she was just an inch shorter than her mother. At the same time, she began to play sports and to hike more, and she began to lose her plumpness. People no longer thought of her as the "butter skin" of the family, the cute chubby one, but as a tall, pretty girl with black hair, long legs, and a funny way of wrinkling her nose when something amused her.

"You need to apply yourself more in school, Louise," her mother said one day. "Your reports haven't been good. I know you won't be happy to stay here in the village, as I have. You're curious about the wider world, and to make your way in it, you'll need to do well in school."

"But Mother, why do you say that? All I've ever wanted is to be like you — to raise a family and maybe run the rooming house with you. I'm not so curious about the world as you think."

"Oh yes — I've seen the way you look at the mountains.

In the evenings, when the sun's going down, I know what you're thinking of then. All the lands and countries beyond, the millions of things you haven't seen yet. You're a wanderer, I can tell."

Louise wanted to explain that she wasn't thinking of foreign lands, but of the mountains themselves — of how the setting sun lit up Henry's Hat, where she and Jean-Claude had climbed that day. But she thought it was probably better not to share her secret.

That winter, an expedition formed to try to climb Mont Dax, in an area of the Alps just north of Montier. Three climbers from Canada hoped to be the first to ascend the mountain by the south buttress route (there were several ways up, but the south buttress route was the hardest). Seven years before, a group had almost made it to the summit, only to be driven back by fierce winds and an ice storm. One of the climbers in that party lost six toes to frostbite. In climbing circles, it was often said that Mont Dax by the south buttress was impossible — only a superman could climb the steep, crumbly rock on that side, in the terrible weather usually found there.

One of the few climbers who thought Mont Dax might not be impossible was Jules DeMaistre. He had never climbed it himself, and now, at age fifty-two, he was a little too old; still, he thought a serious effort might succeed. When the Canadian climbers approached him, in February 1951, he declined to lead their group, but he gave them as much information as he could. In particular, he warned them about the bad rock conditions on the last five hundred feet of the south face.

"The rock is like rotten wood," he said, "eaten through by termites. When you grab a knob, it's likely to come off in your hands. By all means, don't climb till June, when the weather gets better. And don't forget to be extra cautious on the part they call *la glissade du diable* (the Devil's Slide), way up close to the top. Here the rock is at its worst, and avalanches are always sweeping down. Several parties have come to grief there, in view of the summit."

At the end of June, the Canadians set forth, guided by a man named Edouard Bruzel. (Louise was to get to know Bruzel quite well later on — their paths crossed several times in the mountains, sometimes with unpleasant results.) From the first, the Canadian party was plagued by mishaps, mistakes, and miscommunication. It wasn't that the climbers were inexperienced, but Bruzel had been careless in some of his planning: he had bought, for instance, the cheapest hauling ropes he could find, thinking to save a few francs that way. But when the party tried hauling its gear up from base camp, one of the ropes broke, and valuable equipment was lost. Even so, it looked like they might make it to the top. The weather was good, and though they climbed slowly, it seemed that they would have sufficient supplies to stay on the mountain long enough. But then their luck took a turn for the worse.

Bruzel, climbing in the lead one morning, stepped on a rotten slab of rock. It broke, and he fell twenty feet to a ledge below. Though not seriously injured, he had twisted his ankle, and he decided to rest for a while. The Canadians wanted to continue, but they were shy about arguing with their guide. If he said it was okay to waste a day resting, then they had to agree. Everyone made himself as comfortable as possible on the ledge, waiting for Bruzel's ankle to feel "just a little better, just a little bit."

The next day, Bruzel hauled himself to his feet and started up again. But the beautiful weather of the previous three days was gone. Instead of a bright blue sky, the party faced angry, dismal skies of a peculiar gray-yellow color. The Canadians had never seen such a sky before. They asked Bruzel what it meant, but he shook off their questions as "the mewing of scared kittens."

"If I can climb on this miserable ankle," he said, "surely you can climb without whining and complaining. I tell you, the weather will hold — we only have to make it up another thousand feet. Then we're at the bottom of the Devil's Slide. From there it's easy."

"No," one of the Canadian climbers responded, "not so easy — not easy at all. Monsieur DeMaistre said that the Devil's Slide was the most dangerous part. He said to be extra careful there."

"If Monsieur DeMaistre is so wonderful," Bruzel replied acidly, "why has he remained in Montier, in his comfortable house, while I've agreed to lead you? Can you tell me that? I'll hear no more of the great Jules DeMaistre, if you don't mind. Simply follow me, and you'll soon find yourselves at the summit."

The muddy yellow sky, growing thicker by the minute, seemed to press down on them. The temperature dropped twenty degrees in half an hour, and a sullen wind, bearing the scent of snow, blew down from the direction of the summit. Just as the Devil's Slide was coming into view, a cold rain started to fall. In another minute it turned to snow.

This was a wet, heavy snow — very slippery underfoot, chilling, treacherous. Edouard Bruzel brought his party into a small cave, where the overhanging rocks protected them from the moisture. But it was cold inside that cave. All the climbers, sweaty from their recent exertions, became chilled as they sat.

"We can't stay here," one of them said finally. "We're shivering, and in a while we'll all start getting sleepy. That's a sign of serious problems — exposure and so on."

"Break out the sleeping bags, then!" Bruzel shouted. "Wrap yourselves up! Do I have to do everything for you? Are you a bunch of sniveling babies?"

Unfortunately, the sleeping bags were lost. They were in the gear sack that fell down the mountain when the hauling rope broke. When Bruzel realized this, he became even more unpleasant than before. He cursed the mountain and the weather, as well as the hauling ropes and the missing sack.

"The weather will break, I guarantee it," he said sometime later. "I've seen storms like this before. In June it only snows for a half hour, an hour at most. But oh, my blasted ankle! You don't know how it hurts — this foul weather makes it throb like crazy!"

They waited an hour — then another hour. The snow continued piling up outside the cave, while inside, the three climbers, plus their heroic guide, all huddled together to share the warmth of their bodies. And now an unexpected danger made itself known. Every few minutes, an avalanche swept down the face of Mont Dax. (This is why the area of the mountain is known as the Devil's Slide, because the ledges of snow near the summit are always breaking off and tumbling down the south face.) If the climbers hadn't been protected inside the cave, they would surely have been knocked off the mountain by these avalanches.

"What can we do? Oh, what can we do?" Bruzel exclaimed, with a wild look in his eyes. Then turning to the Canadians he said, "Yes — you keep asking me what to do. Well, I'll tell you: we have to sit here, stay calm, not move a muscle! Do absolutely nothing! I'll lead us out of here — I'll get us to the summit!"

Somehow, these reassurances had a contrary effect. The Canadians looked at one another, swallowed hard, and began to say silent prayers. Meanwhile, outside the cave, the snow kept falling, steadily falling. . . .

Four

While Bruzel and the Canadians were trapped in the cave, Jules DeMaistre was standing on the balcony of his house in Montier, looking up toward the mountains. He could see dark clouds swirling around the summit of Mont Dax.

"Clouds of such thickness, such an evil darkness — it must be snow. But if those four are still climbing, they're in a lot of trouble. Pretty soon the avalanches will be starting. Right up there, on the Devil's Slide."

As a mountain guide, Jules DeMaistre had often led parties to rescue stranded or injured climbers. He was just wondering if such an effort was needed now, when there came a tremendous pounding at his front door.

"Papa, it's Monsieur Leval!" called Jean-Claude. "He's asking if you'll lead a rescue party! Some crazy Canadians have gotten themselves stuck on the south buttress!"

"Yes, I expected as much," DeMaistre shouted downstairs. "Tell Leval I'll be there in a minute. As soon as I get my pants on."

DeMaistre agreed to lead the rescue. But he thought the situation might already be hopeless. Just two years before, a party of climbers had gotten stuck in the same area. All attempts to reach them had failed.

"To get near the Slide, you have to approach from below or, just possibly, from the east ridge. But the eastern side is equally difficult. Only a couple of people have ever climbed it. It takes great skill and luck."

"I can climb it!" exclaimed Jean-Claude. "Please, Papa — take me along with you!"

"No, it's out of the question. I'll climb it myself, Jean-Claude. With Leval seconding me on the rope."

"But Papa — you don't know how good I am! I've been climbing all along! Just last fall, I climbed Henry's Hat. It was easy for me. . . ."

DeMaistre looked coldly at his son. He had known that Jean-Claude was going on "unscheduled" climbs; he even suspected that Louise, his daughter, had accompanied her brother once or twice.

"The fact that you disobeyed me," DeMaistre said evenly, "isn't so important. But admitting it this way, bragging about your accomplishments, shows a serious lack of judgment. The one thing a climber needs is good judgment. All the rest can be learned, but a climber's either born with good sense or he isn't."

"But Papa . . . I didn't mean . . . that is, I —"

"Enough!" DeMaistre shouted. "Go to your room now! When I come back from this rescue, we'll have further words on this subject. Yes — I can guarantee that!"

While DeMaistre got ready to leave, Jean-Claude retreated to his room. Louise heard him in there half an hour later, banging around in frustration.

"What's the matter?" she asked through the closed door. "Sounds like you're wrecking the place, Jean-Claude. Can I come in?"

"No! Go away! I'm about to do something really desperate. I'll show him — you bet I will!"

Twenty minutes later, Louise saw her brother leaving the house by the rear door. He had a yellow climbing rope coiled over his shoulder, and on his back was an old leather rucksack. She watched him disappear quickly into the woods.

"No, it can't be," she thought. "He wouldn't dare. . . ."

But the more she thought about it, the more worried she became. Quickly dressing in her climbing clothes, she sneaked downstairs. Without telling her mother, she slipped out the same back door, following her brother up into the woods.

Three hours later, high on the slopes of Mont Dax, Jules DeMaistre pulled himself onto an icy ledge. The snow had stopped falling. But there was a coating of ice on all the rocks, just enough to make holding on extremely difficult. On the climb to this point, DeMaistre had lost his grip several times, and he considered himself lucky to have made it this far.

When his climbing partner, Leval, joined him on the ledge, DeMaistre said:

"We'll set up a belay here, Maurice. We can't climb any farther without ropes to protect us."

Leval agreed. "Yes, I almost bought it on that last pitch. Have you thought about what to do if we can reach the Slide? How to get the bodies down, for instance?"

"You assume they're already dead, Maurice. Don't be so pessimistic. The Canadians are being led by Edouard Bruzel. Though he's not someone I respect, he's a clever old fellow. To say the least, he has a strong interest in his own good health. It takes more than a snowfall to kill that type."

A thousand feet above them, the Devil's Slide was just coming into view. DeMaistre and Leval had climbed the east ridge of Mont Dax, and their approach left them a few hundred yards to the right of the Slide. Looking up, DeMaistre saw a small avalanche just then sweeping down the face.

"If they got caught in one of those, they're gone. I haven't seen any sign of them. But I remember a few caves in that area. Maybe they've taken cover."

"Let's hope so," Leval answered doubtfully.

The hardest part of their climb was just ahead. To get to where the Canadians might be required a traverse of about three hundred yards. There was almost nothing to hold on to, and the few tiny ledges were slick with new ice.

Looking straight down, DeMaistre saw the town of Montier thousands of feet below; he could just make out his own house, shrunk to the size of a bread crumb.

"We need protection here," DeMaistre said over his shoulder. "I'll attach the rope to the rocks, then climb out farther."

"All right. But be careful, Jules — I don't like the look of it."

As DeMaistre edged out to his left, he felt the rock shift under his feet. This was some of that rotten, unstable rock for which Mont Dax is well known. It occurred to him that the covering of ice might actually work in their favor: to a certain extent it held the rocks in place, froze them solid to one another. As long as the sun didn't melt the ice, the traverse they were on might be possible.

After half an hour of difficult, slippery climbing, DeMaistre reached the area directly under the Slide. The caves where the Canadians might be were above, forty yards straight up. But now he saw something that caused his blood to run cold. A hundred yards below and to the right, two climbers were clawing their way up a steep, icy stretch of the mountain wall.

"Who can that be?" he thought. "Who'd be so crazy as to come out today, when the rocks are covered with ice?"

Now Leval caught up with DeMaistre. He, too, noticed the climbers below them.

"Who can that be? Why, they're completely mad, Jules! They'll never make it — that part of the wall has never been climbed, as far as I know."

As the two men watched, the two other climbers — Jean-Claude and Louise, of course — came to rest on a slanted ledge. Though DeMaistre recognized them now, he still couldn't believe what he was seeing: his own children, aged fifteen and thirteen, climbing one of the most dangerous routes in the Alps. Even more astonishing, it was young Louise, not her older brother, who was leading on the rope. (She had taken over from Jean-Claude when, as had happened on Henry's Hat, he reached a part of the cliff he couldn't manage.) Louise, apparently, was the more agile of the two, better at keeping her balance on tiny, slippery footholds.

"Jules," Leval whispered, "I'm afraid that those two youngsters are your own —"

"Yes, yes, I know. And please — don't speak too loudly. You might startle them."

After a short rest, the young climbers continued up. It was clear to DeMaistre that they were completely exhausted, that only a combination of fear and desperation was keeping them from falling off. Having come more than halfway up the mountain, they now realized that their only chance lay in making it to the top. To climb back down would have been harder — maybe impossible.

"When they reach that shattered boulder," DeMaistre whispered, "I'm going to call out. But I'm going to speak calmly, as if it were the most natural thing in the world to run into them up here, on this terrible, icy face."

When he saw Louise at the boulder, DeMaistre called down to his daughter. He asked her in a cheerful voice if she had remembered to bring him up some chocolate — he was getting hungry, he said, and it was still hours till dinnertime. At the sound of her father's voice, an expression of fear, surprise, and deep relief crossed Louise's face. Until that moment, she had believed that she would never see him again — that she and her brother were doomed to die on this terrible cliff, which they had mistakenly thought they could climb.

"Papa! Oh — Papa! I don't know what to do! I'm so scared. And Jean-Claude has cut his hand badly, and we're very tired. . . ."

Just then, Jean-Claude reached the boulder, too. DeMaistre could see that his hand was wrapped in a piece of bloody cloth. Jean-Claude was equally surprised to see his father above them — so surprised, that he almost lost his grip and fell.

"Careful!" his father shouted anxiously. "Quickly, tie yourselves in to the rock! I can't believe you've climbed all this way without belaying. Be calm now; don't do anything foolish, and I'm sure we'll get out of this alive."

When his two children were attached to the cliff, DeMaistre dropped a rope down to the shattered boulder. Then he carefully climbed down. He examined Jean-Claude's hand. Two of the boy's fingers looked broken, and there was a deep cut across the back of his hand.

"You'll be all right," he said. "But we have to keep climbing — on up to the caves. Think you can do it?"

"Y-y-yes," Jean-Claude said uncertainly.

"You've done well so far. No one has ever climbed this

route before, did you know that? But tell me: has Louise been leading the whole time? Or just since you hurt your hand?"

"Well . . . not *quite* the whole time," the boy answered slowly. "There was a smooth patch of rock, you see, very icy and steep, and I had trouble getting up. Louise isn't bothered by things like that. Oh, Papa — I'm *so* sorry! I don't know why I did this crazy thing! I'll never disobey you again, never! I promise!" And then he started to cry.

DeMaistre comforted his son, and he tied him on to his own climbing rope. He urged Jean-Claude to begin climbing to the higher ledge. The boy went at a painfully slow pace, but eventually he arrived. Then it was Louise's turn. She climbed much faster, with little show of difficulty.

"Very good," their father called up. "Now follow Leval's instructions. I'll climb behind you, bringing the yellow rope."

By slow, careful progress, the party made its way up. Just before dark they arrived at a tiny cave, so small that they couldn't all squeeze into it together. DeMaistre had to spend the night outside, huddled on a ledge. The cave with the Canadians was just above, only about fifty feet away. However, neither party was aware of the other, and everyone passed a cold, uncomfortable night.

Five

In the Canadians' cave, conditions had worsened steadily. From the back of the cave came a strong current of cold air, as if the mountain were constantly blowing its icy breath on them. Though lying together for warmth, the three climbers and one guide were miserably uncomfortable — wet, half-frozen, and scared.

"We have to try for the top today," one said. "We can't survive another night like this. Brian can't feel his toes anymore. And Mark keeps shivering, and his hands are blue."

The guide, Edouard Bruzel, had crawled to the front of the cave. With his head stuck out cautiously, he looked up and down the cliff.

"Did you hear me?" the young climber asked. "I said: we have to try for the top. To stay in this cave means certain death."

"Just do as I tell you!" Bruzel answered unpleasantly. "I've brought you this far — I'll lead you the rest of the way, too. To try the face today would be suicide. The Slide is full of fresh snow, and it'll be coming down in avalanches. You don't want to be swept off, do you? Well — do you?"

"No. But I'd rather be killed by an avalanche, if it came to that, than freeze to death in this foul cave. It'd be quicker."

They had had nothing to eat in two days. Even more important, they had had nothing to drink, and the lack of fluids in their bodies was making them feel weak, confused. They might have reached outside the cave and pulled in snow to melt; but Bruzel, who should have thought of this, was too concerned with his own safety. He had calculated that the guides down in Montier would know by now that a party was in trouble on the cliff. In a few hours, they would send up a rescue party, or maybe they would lower ropes from the summit. Then he, Bruzel, could get off the mountain without much effort or risk.

"No," he said, "we'll simply stay where we are. The weather looks threatening, anyway. Could be another storm coming."

"I don't know what you're talking about!" the young climber cried suddenly. "The sky's perfectly clear. There's not a breath of wind, either. Yesterday you said it wouldn't snow, and it did. Today the sky's blue, and you're afraid to try the face. I don't understand you!"

"Never say that I am afraid!" Bruzel screamed in reply.

"Never! I don't flinch in the face of danger, no, I never have! Not once in a life spent entirely in the mountains!"

At just that moment — as Bruzel, red in the face, was shaking a fist at the young Canadian — there came an unexpected sound. A mountain-climbing rope, as it slides through a metal clip called a carabiner, makes a certain tinkling, bell-like sound; and this is what the stranded climbers suddenly heard.

The Canadian rushed to the mouth of the cave. Looking down, he saw an amazing sight.

A young girl, hardly more than a child, was steadily climbing up the rock face. A rope was tied around her waist, and on her back she carried a leather rucksack. (Louise had taken over Jean-Claude's rucksack, to make it easier for him to climb with his injured hand.) The morning sunlight shone on her thick, blue-black hair, and her pretty lips were pursed in concentration.

"Papa!" the girl called down. "I've reached a sort of ledge. But I don't see any other caves. No — there's nothing up here."

Just then, she lifted her gaze. Her dark eyes widened in surprise — the young Canadian was only a few yards above her.

She smiled, and then she called back down to her father: "Wait, I take that back! There *are* some other caves. And it looks like one of them is inhabited."

Louise climbed the last few yards, and the Canadian reached down and took her by the hand. Then he pulled her into his cave. In a few minutes, Jules DeMaistre also arrived, followed in short order by Jean-Claude and Leval. Now the cold, gloomy cave was much warmer, filled as it was with eight spirited, happy people. Greetings were offered all around, and Leval and DeMaistre distributed food and water to the needful Canadians.

"Jules DeMaistre!" Bruzel said enthusiastically. "Why, it's Jules DeMaistre! *Most* pleased to meet you! Yes, most pleased! I've followed your illustrious career for many years. And now I have the honor of meeting you!"

"I've heard of you too, Bruzel," DeMaistre replied evenly; and the way he said this suggested that he, for one, considered it something less than an honor.

After a discussion of the situation, everyone agreed that a new route to the summit had to be designed. The young Canadian thought it might be possible to traverse to the right, away from the area under the Slide, and then to push straight for the top. But DeMaistre said that the rock to the right was even more crumbly. It made more sense to traverse the other way, to the left. He proposed that two climbers venture out, and as soon as they found themselves clear of the avalanche bank, they should make their way to the top.

"Of course, *I'd* like to be one of those lucky two," said Bruzel. "Unfortunately, though, I sprained my ankle just two days ago. It hasn't healed yet. So I'm not at the top of my form."

"I'll climb in your place then," answered DeMaistre. "And if no one has any objection, I'd like to take my daughter, Louise, with me. She can handle the ropes, and her light weight may work to our advantage. When we reach the top, we'll lower a line to the cave. Then you follow us up."

Out on the face of Mont Dax — two thousand feet up in the air — DeMaistre began to have second thoughts. The Slide loomed over them, dangerously banked with fresh snow. If an avalanche came down before they climbed to the left, they were doomed. They had to go a hundred yards on a scary, dangerous traverse in just a few minutes.

"Don't look down, Louise," he said to his daughter. "Don't even think about where we are, and don't look up at the snowbank, either. Just imagine that we're practicing traversing on the stone wall of the church in Montier."

"All right, Papa. Wherever you go, I'll follow. But please — let's hurry."

About fifty yards out, they heard a rumbling above. DeMaistre flattened himself against the rock, and Louise followed his example. Several tons of snow cascaded over them, but as they happened to be standing under an overhanging rock, they weren't swept off. When DeMaistre saw that Louise was all right, he continued traversing.

After twenty minutes, they had climbed clear of the Devil's Slide. And now came a huge, thundering avalanche, much bigger than the one before; it swept past them with only a few yards to spare. If they had been in their previous position, even with the protecting overhang, they would have been pushed to their deaths.

"Don't think about it," DeMaistre said calmly. "It happens sometimes in the mountains that you live . . . or you don't. All you can do is climb as well as you can, take precautions, and hope for luck. Oh yes — and pray."

After two hours of hard, vertical climbing, they reached the summit. DeMaistre was full of admiration for his daughter, who had climbed this route without complaint and with an ease and grace that he had never seen before in a young climber. They lowered safety lines back down the cliff, and DeMaistre and Leval led the Canadian party, plus Jean-Claude, out from under the Devil's Slide and up to the top. By the third of July (two days after the beginning of the rescue effort), everyone was safely back in Montier.

Six

On the night of July 5, just before his group left Montier, the young Canadian asked Louise to go for a walk.

"Up in the mountains again?" she said, smiling. "Haven't you had enough?"

"No. I can't ever get enough of the mountains. Let's go see the sunset from that hill over there. I have something to say to you."

Louise was curious about what he had to say. The Canadian's name was Lawrence Darnley, and over the last few days she had gotten to know him a little, and she liked him. He was twenty-two years old. He reminded her of her brother Rifi: he was tall and thin, like Rifi had been, but very strong, with curly hair the color of old bricks. Of the three Canadians, he was the friendliest and funniest, and only he seemed really disappointed that their climb up the Devil's Slide hadn't succeeded.

"My two friends don't really care," he explained. "They've had a lot of chances to climb in the Alps. This is Brian's tenth trip to Europe, and Mark, whose father is one of the richest men in Quebec, can fly over whenever he wants. But I've had to work and save for three years just to pay for this trip. And it may be my last, too — in September I'm going back to school, to medical school. I have four years of studying ahead of me."

"Well, when you get to be a doctor, you'll have lots of money," Louise replied. "Then you can come over all the time. If you're worried about someone else climbing the Direct before you, don't be too concerned. No one else even wants to try. It's too dangerous."

"That's what they said about all the famous routes. That they were too hard — too dangerous. But someone with guts always manages to go up them! I've been thinking about climbing the Devil's Slide since I was little. I used to read about it in my books on Alpine adventures: the Freitag party — the Winkler attempt — the DeGrazi expedition, when they reached the caves, only to be wiped out in a rockslide. Six men lost! What a tragedy! That mountain's a killer, but it can be climbed. I'm sure of it!"

When talking about things other than Mont Dax, Lawrence was easygoing, and Louise asked about his life back home. Did he come from Quebec, too? (No, from Montreal.) Where had he learned to speak French so well? (His mother was of French descent, his father English.) Did he have brothers and sisters? Were they as interested in mountain climbing as he was?

"No. I only have one brother, and he works in a bank. He says I'm crazy to climb. My parents aren't happy about it, either. My mother worries a lot. She'd feel better if I were interested in something else — stamp collecting, for example."

Louise wanted to ask him about other things, too. Did he have a girlfriend back home? (She knew it was none of her business, but she was curious anyway.) When he became a doctor, was he going to go on living in Canada? Or was he going to move to France; after all, then he could climb in the Alps whenever he wanted.

But though she was full of such questions, somehow she couldn't make herself say them out loud. Something about Lawrence Darnley made her feel self-conscious; it must have been that he was so much older — and so good-looking. When he smiled in a certain way, she was sure that he was about to tease her; and if he had, she didn't think that she could have stood it.

"What I wanted to say," he finally began, "was just that I . . . well, that I think you're a wonderful climber. I've never seen anything like the way you went up that wall with your father. Even old Bruzel was impressed; what he said was, 'Not so bad, not so bad — if she wasn't a girl, she might even make a mountaineer some day.' "

"Oh, is *that* what he said?"

"Don't be offended. He's just an old-timer, Louise — as well as a bit of a cheat. He made us pay double the going rate, because we were on the mountain an extra two days; but it was your father who saved us, wasn't it? Anyway, he doesn't think girls belong in the mountains. I guess most of the old guides feel that way — they don't think girls are strong enough. But you're a special case, Louise. You were made for this kind of thing. You're your father's daughter, no doubt about it."

Despite these words of praise, Louise felt a little disappointed. Was this all that he had wanted to tell her? To say that he admired her rock-climbing skills? Nothing more?

"And . . . if you're still interested in climbing in a couple of years, and if I can manage to somehow —"

His ruddy face turning even redder than usual, Lawrence now stammered out a proposal. In two years' time, if he could get the necessary money and equipment together, he was going to make another attempt on Mont Dax. He thought that a smaller party — a party of just two, or maybe three — would have a better chance of success. He wanted to know if Louise would be his rope partner on that expedition.

"Me? You want me to climb with you? But — I could never do that. You need someone strong and experienced, like my father. You'd better ask him instead."

"But I don't want to climb with your father," Lawrence answered quickly. "It's *you* I want to go with. And I know we can do it, too. I saw how you climbed three days ago. In a few years' time, you'll be that much bigger and stronger. I'm *sure* we can succeed — absolutely sure!"

Despite herself, Louise was flattered to be asked to come. She doubted that her father would give his permission, so she didn't take the idea too seriously; still, it was fun to pretend, to dream that it might happen one day. She told the Canadian that she would consider his offer, but that he shouldn't count on her coming. This next fall, she would be going away to boarding school in Grenoble. She might forget all about climbing after studying there awhile.

"No," he answered, "I don't think you'll ever forget about the mountains. They're in your blood — just as they're in mine. You don't have to decide right now, Louise. And in two or three years, when I return to France, we'll see how things look for us both."

Half an hour later, as they were walking back toward the rooming house, Lawrence casually took her hand. He did this so naturally, with so little fuss, that Louise hardly noticed — it was as if her father or brother had taken her hand while they were walking to church on Sunday. But later that night, as she was lying in her bed, thinking of the events of the last few days, she remembered holding Lawrence's hand — and this thought filled her with a kind of warm confusion.

Seven

The next two years were the loneliest and unhappiest of Louise's life. She moved to Grenoble in September 1951 to begin studying at the Académie Ponséart, a boarding school for girls. Many famous Frenchwomen, actresses and professors among them, had attended the Académie, and though they all spoke fondly of the school in later years, as students they had often been miserable. The school emphasized hard work and strict discipline, and the course of study included French, Latin, Greek, German, physics, and chemistry. Not to mention geometry, trigonometry, world history, and biology; philosophy, economics, political science, and "logical expression" (Louise's least-favorite class). She felt burdened down by all the schoolwork, but she was even more unhappy about being away from her family. She missed her mother and father terribly. She missed her older sister, and she even missed Jean-Claude, who had often teased her and gotten her into trouble.

She wrote her mother a letter when she had been at school only a month, begging to be allowed to come home. But she never mailed that letter. Her father's last words to her, as he said good-bye at the tram stop in Montier, had been: "We know you'll do well, Louise — you've always made us so proud. It may be hard at first, but stick it out. We DeMaistres have a stubborn streak. We don't give up easily. May God protect you. . . ."

How could she quit, then, and disappoint them all — especially considering how expensive the school was? She had won a partial scholarship, but her mother and father were saving every extra franc to pay her way. Jules DeMaistre had even started guiding again (he had retired several years before) and was once more leading some of the most difficult, most dangerous routes.

She had one close friend at the Académie, a girl named Isabel de Clermont-Ferrand, who came from one of the oldest families in France. Isabel's father was a marquis and owned thousands of acres of farmland (there is even a city in central France — Clermont-Ferrand — named after a distant ancestor). Isabel was a good student, but what she really liked was the outdoors. In a roomful of girls suffering through a Latin test, she would always be the first to finish, so she could run outside and lie down on the grass in the courtyard. Or when a vacation came, she would always be sure to plan a hike, a skiing trip, or a swim in the nearby lakes. Louise often went on these trips of Isabel's. They had this one thing in common, that they preferred to be outdoors, with the sky above them and real earth (or mountain granite) under their feet; and they endured their academic duties, rather than actually enjoyed them.

"Louise, you're crazy!" exclaimed Isabel in the middle of their second school year. "You *have* to tell your father how unhappy you are. I don't think I've seen you smile in three months."

"That's not true, Isabel. I did some smiling in February, when we went up in the hills on our skis. And I'll be smiling again in April, when we go on that canoe trip. But for now I see nothing to smile about. I have thirty irregular verbs to conjugate in German. Then I have to write an essay in English, do pages of math problems, and study for a test in physics."

"You take things too seriously, Louise. Life isn't only about irregular verbs. Just relax. Don't get that gloomy look on your forehead. You always do well on your tests anyway, so why worry? Just be happy."

"But I'm *not* happy, Isabel. Every day I wake up and wish I was back in Montier. At this time of year, there're fifteen feet of snow on the ground, and it's so cold you can hear the air snap, like glass. My mother's baking bread for the guests in the hotel kitchen, and my brother's probably out skiing all over. Meanwhile, my father's sitting by the fireplace on the second floor, smoking his smelly pipe, slowly going over his climbing equipment with his big, scarred hands. . . ."

That April, the girls went on a canoe trip with some friends. The river they were canoeing ran through a deep gorge, with sheer cliffs rising up on either side. As they came to a sandbank in the river, they saw another canoe pulled up, and they decided to take a rest. No sooner had they climbed out of their canoes than they heard frantic calls for help.

"Has someone fallen in the river? Is someone drowning?" Isabel wondered, looking up- and downstream.

"No. The calls are coming from the cliffs over there," Louise said. "But you can't tell which one, because there's so much echoing."

Louise ran down along the sandy bank. Where the river went around a bend, she saw two people high on a cliff. It was a man and a woman; they had started climbing a wide crack in the rock. Soon, though, the crack narrowed, and the cliff became much more steep. Now the people were about two hundred feet up in the air, trapped on a thin ledge.

Isabel and the other girls caught up with Louise. All watched in horror as the man tried to climb out of his dangerous position. He scrambled up a few feet, then lost his grip and slid back down, onto the ledge. He tried again; this time he slid down past the ledge, and he only saved himself by grabbing for his partner's hand.

"Help! Help!" the woman screamed every few seconds. She looked frantically up and down the gorge; she hadn't yet noticed that the girls were at the bottom of the cliff, directly below her position.

"We're down here!" Louise called up. "We'll help you! But you have to stop trying to climb — don't move at all, just stay right there. I'll be up in a minute."

Each of the canoes had come equipped with a short length of cord. Louise tied these quickly together, making a rope about forty feet long.

"But what are you thinking of, Louise?" asked Isabel. "You're not going to climb up there, are you? Why — that's insane! Those people are in a bad position, and what's worse, they're in a panic. As soon as you get close they'll grab for you. Then you'll all fall."

Louise assured Isabel that nothing of the sort was going to happen. She had spotted a way to get to the top from the ledge; she would climb up, then simply show them the way.

"But Louise — I won't let you go! You don't know how dangerous it is. You can't climb without a belay. These little bits of cord won't protect you, you know that."

"I don't need protection, Isabel," Louise answered calmly. "I could make it up that crack with my eyes closed." And then she smiled — a big, reassuring smile, warm and happy. "Don't worry, Isabel. This is how I have my fun. My idea of a good time is climbing steep rocks — not conjugating some old German verbs, or anything like that. . . ."

Halfway up the cliff, though, Louise began to have doubts. The climbing was easy, but she was getting close to the people now, and she could see the look of terror in their eyes. Being stranded on a high cliff is a horrifying experience, especially for someone without much knowledge of climbing; you can feel your strength slowly giving out, and you know that death is waiting, patiently waiting for you down below. Louise herself had been stranded several times. Once, when she was seven, she climbed up a steep rock outside Montier, thinking she could make it all the way to the top. In the middle, though, the climbing suddenly became too hard, and she was completely stuck. To go back down was impossible — she couldn't see where to put her feet. Going up was also out of the question; so in the end, she simply started to cry, out of sheer terror. Luckily, her brother Rifi, who happened to be passing near the rocks, heard her and came to her rescue.

"Don't be afraid," she now called up to the climbers. "I'm going to help you," she said in a soothing voice. "Just try to relax. Take some deep breaths, and try to think of something pleasant."

The woman climber, who was only a few yards above, turned to her partner and said, "This girl must be completely crazy. She just told us to think of something pleasant! Can you imagine? As if I could forget about being two hundred feet in the air, having only a few seconds left to live!"

"No," Louise said, "you don't have just a few seconds left. I'm going to lead you up to the top, and you'll be fine. But first, I want you to calm down a little. Try to stop clinging to each other. You're fairly safe if you stay where you are. I repeat — just stay where you are."

Louise climbed a little closer to the ledge. As she did, the woman let go of the man, and she began edging over toward Louise. Louise didn't like the look on her face: she was smiling strangely, showing her whole mouthful of teeth. It reminded Louise of a picture she had seen once, of a timber wolf about to leap on a fawn.

"Madame — don't come any closer, please. It isn't safe. Now, I'm going to throw you this rope. Don't pull on it, just catch hold of it. Then hand it to your friend."

"All right. Yes, yes — throw me the rope! Throw me the rope, by all means!"

Louise tied one end of the rope to a knob of rock. Now she tossed the rest, in coils, toward the ledge; it landed just at the woman's feet. But instead of bending down to pick it up, the woman lunged, immediately lost her footing, and nearly tumbled over the edge.

"Help me! Oh God — help me!" she screamed hysterically. Half her body now dangled in thin air; the other half clung to the rope and to the ledge.

"Françoise!" the man cried. "Wait — I'm coming, Françoise! I'll save you!"

Louise had to act fast. In another second, the man would have let go his grip, crawled over, and then both might have gone over the edge. Louise moved carefully out of the crack and onto the cliff face. She found a handhold, then another, and in less than thirty seconds, she had reached the ledge.

As soon as the woman felt Louise standing next to her, she let go of the rope. She grabbed desperately for Louise; she caught her around the knees, then hung on with the terrible strength of someone in fear for her life. Louise fell down from her position. In two or three seconds, she was at the edge herself, with the weight of the woman's body forcing her over.

Down on the riverbank, Isabel cried out in alarm. From her position, it looked as if the woman had purposely pulled Louise down from the cliff; now they were wrestling, half tangled up in the rope. And then — Louise fell. Isabel saw her come clear of the rock, turn a somersault in the air, and fall for a distance of about fifteen feet. But then something strange happened. It seemed as if an invisible hand had caught her, jerked her back. She swung over toward the crack, slamming into the wall with great force. A moment later Isabel noticed that the rope, which was tied in the crack, had gotten tangled around Louise's wrist. With her free hand Louise clutched at the rocks, and just as her wrist was slipping out of the rope, she found something to grab.

"Louise! Louise!" Isabel screamed.

There was no answer. For several moments Isabel watched, hardly daring to breathe, as her friend scrambled back to a safe position. Soon she was securely wedged in the crack.

"Yes — I'm okay!" came the call from above. "I hurt my wrist a little. That's all."

Over on the ledge, the man and woman looked across at Louise. The woman, whose panic had almost led to all their deaths, seemed to be sorry for what had happened. She kept shaking her head, and her sobs could be heard even at the bottom of the cliff.

"Louise — please come down! Leave them up there!"

Isabel begged. "We'll get help farther down the river. Don't try to climb any more. Please, just come down."

"I can't," came the answer. "It's harder to climb down, and anyway I can't just leave them here. Give me a few more minutes. I'm going to make one more try. . . ."

Isabel watched Louise climb farther up the crack. Then, once again coiling the rope and tossing it to the ledge, Louise traversed to her left, arriving just above the position of the stranded climbers. Down on the ground, Isabel couldn't hear what Louise was saying; but first the woman, then the man, tied the rope carefully at the waist, and when Louise gestured for them to step back, to make room for her on the ledge, they immediately did so. The three of them remained together for a while — undoubtedly, Louise was giving them instructions on how to follow her — and soon they began to climb up.

After twenty or thirty minutes, they disappeared from view. Louise had found a second crack, to the left of the ledge, which slanted toward the top. It was up this crack that they made their escape.

Eight

As a result of this adventure — an "amazing and noble rescue," according to the newspapers — many things changed for Louise. Her father visited her in the hospital (she had broken her left wrist, after all), and they had a serious, honest discussion about the Académie Ponséart. Louise said that while she appreciated all her parents were doing, she just didn't feel at home at the school; what she wanted, with all her heart, was to return to Montier. Her father, to her surprise, quickly agreed. Her family missed her as much as she missed them, and he only asked her to finish out the term at school. Then, two months later, she was certified as a *guide aspirant* (apprentice guide) by the Association of Guides of the Massif, which meant that she could help as a porter on expeditions in the local mountains. She was one of the youngest people ever to be certified, as well as the first girl. The local newspapers, which had written about the rescue in the gorge, also wrote about this honor, and Louise began to have a small reputation in French climbing circles.

The man and woman she rescued, wanting to show their appreciation, sent a donation in her name to the Académie Ponséart. (Louise would have preferred a donation to a certain ex-student of the Académie, but she was grateful in any case.)

That summer, she worked harder than ever before in her life. A porter helps on a climb by carrying everything heavy and bulky — extra ropes, clothes, food, gear, sleeping bags. There is a saying in the massif, "A mule has a stable, but a porter sleeps out in the rain." This means that while a mule is a beast of burden, at least someone feeds it, takes care of it; but a porter, also used as a mere beast sometimes, has to look out for himself (or herself). After trudging up steep trails all day, wearing a pack weighing more than fifty pounds, Louise often had to sleep out in the wet and cold. It was considered an important part of her training to be exposed to such conditions — in later years, when leading expeditions herself, she might have to sacrifice her own comfort or, if necessary, her own life. So Louise ate rough food, slept out on the rocks, and carried loads that would have been heavy for a full-grown man. She was only fifteen, but she had grown rather tall by now — she towered over her mother, and she was only a half inch shorter than her older brother, Jean-Claude.

Despite all the work, Louise had a wonderful season. She was happy to be back in the mountains, back with her family, back doing what she loved best. Her only truly harsh experience involved her father's "old friend" (that was what he called himself), the senior guide, Edouard Bruzel. Bruzel, leading a climb on the Dent du Monstre (Monster's Tooth), requested that Louise be assigned to him as porter. He said that he wanted to "take her under my wing, so to speak — see that she isn't being mistreated." But on the hike up to the Dent, he made sure that she had the heaviest, bulkiest pack to carry. Then when she began to lag behind, he loudly announced to the entire party:

"You see, this is what happens when a *girl* does a man's work. She falls behind, she just can't keep up. Pretty girls are all very fine down in the meadows, larking about with flowers in their hair; but please, keep them out of my mountains! They just don't belong!"

Hearing these words, Louise gritted her teeth. She summoned all her strength, and soon she had passed the other porters and climbers and was walking at the head of the line.

"Watch out, my friend," Bruzel warned her. "We have a long distance to go yet. If you get tired and fall behind, I'll report you to the Guides' Association. We can't have our porters interfering with the success of the expedition."

"Monsieur Bruzel," she replied, "I'm interfering with no one, as far as I can see. You may say what you want to the Association — I don't really care. And I know exactly how far it is to the base of the Dent. I've climbed here many times. Probably more often than you, in fact."

"Young lady," said Bruzel, "see that you speak to me in

a civil tone. I'll have no disrespect from you. Just because you have a famous father gives you no right to put on airs. It isn't how big your name is here in the mountains, but how much grit you have. How tough you really are."

Some time later, the party came to the edge of an ice field. On the other side was the base of the Dent, where the actual climbing would begin. One of the porters, needed for another expedition, turned back here. Bruzel picked up the extra pack, and he said:

"Who can carry this load? It isn't so heavy — only about thirty pounds. Come on, come on. I need a volunteer. What about you, Hervet? Can you do it?"

Hervet, another apprentice guide, slowly shook his head. "To be honest, Monsieur Bruzel, I've had a hard time just carrying this single pack. And I know what it's like going across that ice field — the footing's very bad. You could hurt yourself carrying an extra pack. If you please, I'd rather carry the loads one at a time — go across with this one, then come back for the other."

"Oh, is *that* what you're made of?" sneered Bruzel. "Is that what our French youth has come to? When I was young, I carried triple and quadruple packs as a matter of course, and not just across a little ice field, either. On Mont Blanc, we often had to *climb* with double packs. And without being roped up."

As Bruzel described a few other great accomplishments of his youth, Louise quietly went over to pick up the extra pack. But Tricoussan, another of the apprentices, had had the same idea; and as he and Louise bent down to grab it,

Hervet, embarrassed by his earlier refusal, also reached in to get the extra load.

"Oh — what's this?" exclaimed Bruzel. "Now we have *plenty* of volunteers — how nice! But let the young lady have it, Hervet. And you, Tricoussan, step back there; let go of that strap. If she wants it that much, give it to her. Let me help you put it on, my dear."

Bruzel quickly loaded the second pack onto Louise's shoulders. The two packs together made an unwieldy, unbalanced burden; she staggered, almost lost her footing, then righted herself. At first, she thought she wouldn't be able to bear the weight. But after a minute, she became used to it.

Bruzel, who normally walked at a leisurely pace, now set off quickly across the ice field. He was at the front of the party, then came the climbers, then the three apprentice guides. The five climbers, businessmen on holiday from Paris and Grenoble, stopped in the middle of the ice field and threw snowballs at one another. Without any packs to carry, they were having a wonderful time, and they didn't mind slipping and sliding a bit. But Louise and the other porters were in trouble.

Louise slipped once, fell to her knee, then, with help from Tricoussan, slowly stood up again. When they were three-quarters of the way across the field, Tricoussan himself stumbled; Louise went to his aid, but as he was leaning against her, she lost her balance, too. Hervet tried to grab hold of them both, but they ended up sprawled on their backs.

Tricoussan laughed. Louise made no sound, and her face was pinched with pain. She had felt something give way in her knee. She rose up slowly, and at her first step, she cried out.

"What is it?" asked Hervet in alarm. "Did you turn an ankle?"

"No. It's my knee — I sprained it, I think. But I can walk. Yes, come on. We're almost across."

The three covered the remaining width of the ice field without further incident. But that night, when Louise was getting into her sleeping bag, she noticed that her knee was swollen; and when she turned her leg a certain way, a searing pain went through her.

Nine

The next morning, Bruzel sent Tricoussan back, since he needed only two porters to lead the climbers up the Dent. He didn't notice how slowly and carefully Louise moved around camp, but Hervet did; and he asked her how her knee was.

"I can climb, Hervet. Don't worry. I'll be all right."

"Let me see it, Louise. If it's swollen you shouldn't climb. You don't want to make it worse."

"I'm telling you, it's okay, it's okay. And if it *was* swollen, do you think our dear leader would accept that as an excuse? No — he'd tell us about the time he climbed the Eiger with a broken arm, or about how strong he used to be, carrying two-hundred-pound loads."

"Nevertheless," Hervet persisted, "you have to protect yourself. A knee is a delicate thing. If you hurt it, you could ruin your future as a climber. I know — my uncle Fabien, who used to guide in Chamonix, never recovered from a fractured knee. Now he even walks with a cane."

All that morning, Louise climbed with the others. She never complained, but her knee ached continually, and when she made certain movements, a pain like liquid fire shot through her. She avoided making those movements whenever possible, and by early afternoon she was almost comfortable again. The party stopped below the summit to eat lunch. They were on a broad ledge, with a magnificent view of the whole massif. Louise wandered off behind some boulders, and after a few minutes Hervet came after her, to give her a little chocolate.

He found her sitting on a rock, with one leg stretched out in front of her. As he came closer, he heard her crying — then, when she heard him behind her, she stopped crying and pretended just to be blowing her nose.

"What is it, Louise? The knee?"

"Well — it's a little swollen, I guess."

Hervet rolled up her pants leg. He could hardly get the material over her knee: it was swollen to twice normal size. The skin felt very strange, as if there were jelly under it.

"Is it painful, Louise?"

"No. That's what scares me — it hardly hurts anymore, just if I turn it to the right. Then it hurts so bad I feel sick to my stomach."

"Louise, I don't like the looks of it."

"Well, don't tell Bruzel. He'll say I'm making an excuse, that girls can't keep up. I'll wrap it up with my scarf. That should be good enough to get off the mountain."

Despite Louise's request, Hervet immediately reported to Bruzel. The senior guide came back to the boulder to examine her. As soon as he saw her knee, his face became very serious; he sent Hervet to fetch his medical kit, and he wrapped her leg with a gauze bandage, then with the scarf, which he left loose enough for her to walk.

"Go easy — don't put all your weight on it," he advised. "I have an old crevasse stick in my pack; you can use it as a cane. But how did this happen? Did you twist your knee coming up that last pitch?"

"No. I hurt it yesterday. On the ice field."

"On the ice field? Crossing the ice field?" Bruzel looked puzzled, then he began to look nervous. "But why didn't you tell me? It should've been treated last night. And then . . . you were so foolish, Louise. Asking to carry that double pack. I was just fooling when I suggested it . . . everyone knew I was." Turning to Hervet, Bruzel suddenly asked in a pointed way, "Didn't you understand me, Hervet? Wasn't it clear that I was pretending, that I never meant for Louise to do such a crazy thing?"

Hervet looked at Bruzel, then at Louise. Then he looked at Bruzel again. "Well, no," he said. "It wasn't clear. That is —"

"I would *never* require such a thing!" Bruzel suddenly thundered. "My apprentices are too important to me — much too important! Why, it's written in the rules, the rules of the Association, that an apprentice may only carry a single load — 'Only a pack weighing so and so many pounds, and being no larger than this or that many cubic inches,' et cetera. I always protect my young guides. They represent the future of our profession, and we must ensure their safety; we must protect their health above all else. . . ."

Bruzel continued for a while in this vein — about how concerned he was, how deeply anxious about the welfare of his apprentices. At first, Louise didn't understand why he was going on this way. But then she began to see. As usual, he was protecting himself: he was worried about what the Association might have to say. Several times in recent years, when apprentices had sustained bad injuries, the Association had taken disciplinary action against the senior guides in charge. Some guides had paid large fines, while others had actually lost their certificates, which meant that they could never lead expeditions again.

"Monsieur Bruzel," Louise suddenly interrupted. "You don't have to say all this. I'm not going to make trouble for you, I promise. I just want to get off this mountain. Back to where someone can take care of me. I'd like to start climbing down now — can we?"

"Well . . . yes. Certainly. Whatever you say."

And turning to Hervet, Bruzel angrily ordered him to gather up all the equipment, then to go warn the climbers that they were about to start. A certain medical problem had come up, Hervet was ordered to say, and they had to get to a hospital as soon as possible.

Ten

It was fortunate that Louise got down from the Dent as soon as she did. She had injured one of the ligaments in her knee (the anterior cruciate ligament), and if she had continued climbing that day, she might have been permanently crippled. Hervet and two of the climbers carried her into Montier on a stretcher improvised from ice sticks and a sleeping bag. Louise's mother, Martine, immediately put her to bed, and she packed Louise's knee in ice to bring the swelling down. By the time the town doctor arrived, Louise's knee was almost back to normal size, although it ached horribly.

The doctor, an old, red-faced man with a drooping white mustache, declared that she should be taken to Grenoble immediately. "I've seen cases like this before," he said with authority. "She needs an operation, and the sooner the better. If it's successful she'll be walking again in a few months. I know an excellent man in Grenoble, a specialist in orthopedic surgery. He won his reputation during the War, when he performed many amputations. Oh, he was very skillful with the scalpel — a real artist, you might say. I'll call ahead to the hospital. Tell them to get a bed ready."

Martine DeMaistre looked over at her daughter. Louise's eyes were very wide, and her lips were trembling.

"Ummm . . . perhaps we should wait awhile," Martine said to the doctor. "I have to speak to my husband first. He's out on a climb now, leading a party up the Grandes Jorasses. He should be back this evening."

"Whatever you say, Madame," answered the doctor, shaking his head. "Do as you think best. But time is of the essence. Louise should go under the knife within the next few hours, at the latest."

As soon as the doctor left, Louise burst into tears. It was all that talk of amputations that had frightened her, and her mother reassured her by saying that nothing of the sort was in store for her. Then Louise said that she didn't want an operation, she just wouldn't allow it. She was afraid that the doctors would make a mistake, that they would patch her knee up any old way, and that she would never climb again.

"Louise, you heard what the doctor said. I can't believe old Verglace would give us bad advice. When Rifi had scarlet fever that time, he made the correct diagnosis, don't you remember? Then he nursed him back to health."

"Mother, you're wrong about that. It was *you* who nursed Rifi, *you* who brought him back. Dr. Verglace's medicines did nothing — they just cost a lot. It was your herbs and potions that saved Rifi."

Martine DeMaistre shook her head. "I may have helped a little, I don't remember. But it was Dr. Verglace who gave him those funny purple pills, the ones with white stripes. They had a good effect, yes, very good. . . ."

The fact was, Martine DeMaistre was respected as a curer in all the nearby villages. Whenever Dr. Verglace was unavailable, she came to treat sick and injured people, and sometimes she helped them a great deal. Then at other times, her herbal medicines, which she made from plants she gathered herself, had little effect one way or the other.

Now, though, since they had a long wait anyhow (Jules DeMaistre was expected back after supper), Martine went into her little kitchen and began preparing some herbal teas. One of them, with a very bitter taste, immediately made much of Louise's pain go away. She drank two more cups, following her mother's instructions, and she soon became drowsy. Then she fell into a deep, relaxed sleep. While Louise rested, Martine DeMaistre prepared another decoction, a greenish-yellow fluid that smelled like licorice mixed with rusty nails. She applied this to Louise's knee in a warm poultice.

When Jules DeMaistre returned home, he was extremely distressed to see what had happened to his daughter. His wife could only give him vague details about the accident; all she knew was that they were on the Dent, and that Louise had been carrying for Bruzel. As Louise slept on, her mother repeatedly bathed her knee in the strange-smelling potion. Jules and Martine discussed the operation, and just before midnight, Jules slipped out of the house for a little while.

The next morning, Louise felt amazingly better. If her mother had let her, she would have hopped right out of bed, injured knee or no. But Martine insisted that she stay on her back, and all that day (and the next, and the next), Martine applied her poultices. Hervet and Tricoussan came to visit one morning, along with some of Louise's other friends. When they were all standing around, discussing this and that, Tricoussan said casually:

"I went to the guides' office this morning . . . were you there, Hervet? Did you happen to see Bruzel?"

Hervet smiled. "Yes, I did. And I saw his nose, too."

The two apprentices winked at each other. Louise noticed the winks, and she asked them what was so funny.

"Oh — nothing, Louise, nothing really. Why don't you ask someone else about it?" suggested Hervet. "Why not ask your father, for instance?"

"My father? Why should I ask my father?"

"Oh — I don't know."

But after a moment, Hervet explained. The night before last, while he was resting at his parents' house, there came a knock at his window. It was very late — after midnight. Looking out, he saw Jules DeMaistre standing in the yard. He let him in, of course, and Jules explained that he was trying to find out what had happened that day on the Dent. He had already been to see Bruzel. Bruzel had said that Louise's injury was a "simple accident" — she just happened to twist her knee while climbing on some ice.

"And then . . . maybe I shouldn't have, but I told him everything," Hervet continued. "All about the double load. And about how Bruzel got you to carry it, and that *that's* why you slipped, why you hurt yourself. Your father thanked me for the information, then he went off into the night."

"And?" Louise wondered. "Yes — and then?"

"Well" — and again, Hervet smiled at Tricoussan — "when I went down to the guides' office this morning, I ran into Bruzel. And if I'm not mistaken, something has happened to his nose. It's much bigger than it used to be. It's almost as if he ran into a stone wall or something. Or maybe someone hit him with a snowball."

"Yes," Tricoussan put in. "Probably it *was* a snowball. A snowball about as big as a fist."

Louise was puzzled — but then she began to understand. She also began to smile.

"So . . . something has happened to our great leader. How unfortunate. But tell me: did anyone file a report? I don't want him to get in any trouble with the Association. Do you know, did my father file a report?"

"No," said Hervet, "nothing like that."

"Oh, no," Tricoussan agreed. "Your father isn't the sort to file reports. If he wants to discuss something with someone, he does it directly. Yes — as directly as possible."

And then they all began to smile. And though they felt a little embarrassed about it, they soon began to laugh, and quite heartily.

Eleven

The injury to Louise's knee did not, after all, require an operation. After three weeks of bed rest she began exercising again, and soon she was going out on short hikes with her friends. Her mother continued applying herbal poultices, and in late September, only six weeks after her accident, Louise was strong enough to go on a climb with her father and brother.

That winter, when she was sixteen, she worked part-time as a ski instructor. She wore a brace on her knee, but she felt better every day, and by springtime she had begun climbing seriously again. Somehow, her injury had only made her more eager to work hard, to improve; with Jean-Claude, she put up several new routes in the massif, and there was hardly a weekend when they weren't out on the rocks somewhere. She still went to school, at the local lycée, but she had more time now to devote to the outdoors. In addition to climbing, she loved skiing, skating, and ski-touring (cross-country), and her idea of heaven was to combine two or more such activities on one trip (for example, by hiking into the mountains, climbing a cliff with her sticks strapped to her back, then skiing home by a steep downhill route).

Her sister Elise, three years older than Louise, had already gone away to the university. Jean-Claude would probably be going the next year, and it was expected that Louise would follow them. But after another summer as an apprentice guide, she was even surer that she wanted to make her career there in the mountains; that she wanted to become a full-fledged, certified mountain guide, just like her father. There had never been a woman guide before, and some of the seniors, who had thought it charming for a young girl to work as an apprentice, now began to grumble, saying that a woman, no matter how well qualified, simply didn't belong "first on the rope." (The chief guide, the one in charge, generally climbs ahead of the others; this position is the most challenging and dangerous on an expedition.) Louise, hoping to win them over, worked even harder; she never refused a difficult job, no matter how scary or unpleasant, and she never complained. And one by one, the men she worked for began siding with her: after being on dangerous climbs with her, after seeing how brave and competent she was, they felt that she could only bring credit to their profession.

In 1954, while working as a porter on a climb, she met a man named Roger Nicoq, a journalist. Nicoq was tremendously impressed with her skills. He couldn't get over how strong she was, and he wrote a magazine article, with the title "Angels in High Places," that described some of her accomplishments (as well as those of some other female climbers). Though the article had more to say about Louise's "lovely, feminine form," about her "pretty black eyes, full of laughter, but ready to stare death right in the face," than about the actual conditions of life in the mountains, it was read all over France, and she got many friendly letters from other climbers (as well as two proposals of marriage). One of the nicest letters came from someone named Madeleine Duvet, a woman living in Beauvezer, a town not far from Montier. Madeleine invited Louise to come climbing with her that spring.

The river Verdon, which flows past Beauvezer, over the centuries has cut a deep canyon in the earth. This canyon, or gorge, is more than a thousand feet deep in places, and the steep limestone walls offer some of the best climbing in France. Madeleine Duvet had been living here for several years, and she knew the gorge well: she knew which routes were easy, which were terrible, and which "will never be climbed, because you'd have to be crazy even to try them."

On a sunny Sunday in late April, Louise met Madeleine near the gorge, and together they set out to climb some of the popular routes. Madeleine was twenty-four at this time. She had been working as a schoolteacher in Beauvezer, and her husband, also a teacher, was the one who had introduced her to climbing. Together they had pioneered a new route in the gorge — they later named it Le Déjeuner Perdu (The Lost Lunch). Louise thought that this was a peculiar name, but in the middle of the same climb, as she was clinging desperately to a tiny fingerhold, she came to understand the name well. Looking down at the river below, she felt dizzy and sick to her stomach; there was something about the sight of the green water, as it flowed between the sheer, overhanging limestone cliffs, that hypnotized her.

"Louise — are you all right?" Madeleine called out from above.

"Yes. I'm all right. It's just that when I look down, I feel sort of ill."

"Everybody feels funny here, everybody. There's something about that river. It seems to call you, to dare you to jump down. The first time I saw it I really *did* get sick. That's why we gave the climb that name."

When Louise felt better, she followed Madeleine up the pitch, and they rested at the bottom of a narrow chimney in the rock. Madeleine had been leading so far, but now she gave the first position to Louise. The chimney was uncomfortable to climb in. Louise had to wedge herself upward, and the only thing keeping her from falling was the outward pressure of her elbows, knees, and feet.

"It's freezing cold in here," she called down. "There's a trickle of ice water from somewhere, and it's running right down my neck."

Madeleine laughed. "That chimney's a wonderful place,

isn't it? Up ahead it gets even narrower. I hope you're skinny enough to fit through. Bernard, my husband, got caught like a cork in a bottle neck."

Soon Louise arrived at the narrower part. She was just thin enough to fit, but she had a very bad feeling in this place. The walls of icy rock pressed against her, and it was easy to imagine being caught, having the breath slowly squeezed out of her. But when she had wriggled through, she saw light up ahead. She climbed the last fifteen yards quickly, to the top of the wall.

"I made it," she called back down. "Wait a minute, I'll put you on belay. Okay — now it's your turn."

When they were both on top, Louise again looked down to the river. The water made a sort of whirlpool directly below her, and indeed, the circular movement of the green current seemed to invite her, to coax her to let go. She remembered something her father had once said: even experienced guides were subject to spells of vertigo, of dizziness and confusion. The best thing to do when you felt this way, her father had said, was to relax, breathe normally, and look at something close to hand. Staring down into bottomless space was always a mistake, or as DeMaistre called it, an "indulgence"; a professional guide had to control himself at all times, resist such urges.

"Well — how did you like The Lost Lunch?" Madeleine asked.

"Super. Scary, but beautiful, too. Do we have time for another? I'd like to climb something else, something just as upsetting. . . ."

* * *

On the western wall of the Verdon Gorge, at the point of its greatest depth, there is another climb with a funny name. Four months after Louise's first visit to the gorge, she attempted this route. Because she was the first person ever to climb it, she had the right to name it as she wanted.

Le Mur aux Nu-pieds (The Barefoot Wall, as she called it) is about twelve hundred feet high. It begins at the river, on a tiny ledge, and for the first five hundred feet follows a thin, meandering crack in the wall. Down near the water, this crack is wide enough for a climber to fit hands and feet inside. The climbing, while strenuous, is simple in a technical sense — all someone has to do is jam hands and feet in, then move up.

Three hundred feet above the water, though, the crack gets narrower. Now the climber can no longer fit his feet inside, and after a while, even his hands are too big. Louise and Madeleine, being women, had a slight advantage in this respect: their hands were smaller than a man's. But even so, soon they could only get a few fingers in the crack. And then — only fingertips.

"Louise, I don't know," Madeleine called up. "Maybe this is just too hard."

"Well, it's pretty hard, all right," Louise answered. "At the moment I'm holding on by a fingernail, I think. If only I wasn't wearing these stupid boots — then I could do something with my feet, too."

In those days, rock-climbers wore heavy leather boots. The flexible shoes of modern times, with sticky rubber soles, hadn't been invented yet. The shoes Louise was wearing that day weighed over three pounds apiece.

"I think I'd better tie off here, Madeleine," Louise called down. "My arms are getting tired, and I don't know how to go on from here."

"All right — whatever you say."

Louise drove a piton into the rock. With the protection of the rope, which she attached to the hole in the piton, she could rest safely for a moment.

Madeleine climbed up from below. She had even more trouble in the crack; it took all her strength just to reach Louise's position.

"I'm finished," she gasped. "My arms are killing me. Should we rappel down, Louise? I'm afraid that if we go any higher, we'll get stuck. From here at least it's a clear drop to the water."

"Maybe we should turn back," Louise answered uncertainly. "A rappel from here would work without much problem. . . ."

As they rested on their precarious perch, with the river, once again, seeming to invite them to jump, Louise remembered something from long ago. Back in Montier, when she was a little girl, her older brother, Rifi, sometimes used to take her, Jean-Claude, and Elise down to the local quarry. On the hottest days of the summer it was great fun to swim there, in the deep pool that formed in one of the abandoned gravel pits. She remembered how Rifi used to dive in on one side, swim across, and climb out; then, dressed in nothing but his bathing trunks, he would climb up the smooth, overhanging wall on the other side. When he reached the top, he would simply dive back down into the cool, blue-green water.

"Madeleine, isn't it awfully hot today? Wouldn't you just love to jump in that river?"

"Jump?" Madeleine exclaimed. "What — are you crazy? It's a fall of three hundred feet, Louise. We'd kill ourselves."

"Yes, probably. But even so. . . ."

Then — to Madeleine's disbelief — Louise began taking off her boots. She took off her socks, too, and her sweater; but rather than leap into space, she suddenly turned to face the limestone wall. Slipping one finger into the tiny crack above her, she began climbing. With her feet out of the clumsy boots, she could sometimes slip a toe or two into the crack as well. Her progress was slow, and Madeleine could tell that it was also painful: Louise wasn't used to using her feet this way, pinching her toes in the rough, unyielding limestone. But the stability she gained with her feet was useful, and soon she had climbed a whole rope length above Madeleine's position.

"It works!" she shouted down. "It really does! Come on, Madeleine. Give it a try."

"I don't think I want to, Louise. I'm not as nimble as you are. And it would hurt too much."

"Whatever you say, but you have to come up! I can't leave you in the middle of the wall. Start climbing and I'll haul you up on the rope. Come on — don't be lazy."

In this way, with Louise hauling her from above, Madeleine began to climb. She slipped several times, but Louise always caught her with the rope. Soon she had joined Louise on a little ledge.

"We've made it! Look, Madeleine — it's easy from here to the top. I can even put my boots back on. Now, where did I leave them . . . ?"

Unfortunately, Louise had left her boots down at the last belay stance. She looked down the cliff — yes, there they were, her heavy leather boots, looking rather forlorn seventy feet below. Not for anything would she have climbed down the crack again, pinching her toes all the way.

"It looks like I have to stay barefoot — do the whole route without shoes. I don't really mind, though. I sort of like the feel of the rock on my bare feet, to tell the truth. You're like a monkey — you have great control."

At the top of the climb, Louise was in pretty bad shape. Her toes were bruised and bloody, and she had to limp away from the top of the gorge. But she had succeeded in climbing The Barefoot Wall, and in the record books, she is given sole credit for the first ascent.

Twelve

"I'm sorry, I just don't think it's safe."

"But, Louise — you have to try! At least you have to try!"

"If you'd arrived in July, Lawrence, I'd have been happy to go. But now it's snowing up there. The nights are freezing. Our chances aren't good, and every day they get worse."

It was the twenty-seventh of August, 1956. Lawrence Darnley, the young Canadian doctor (he had finished medical school just two months before), had returned to France. He was determined to climb the Devil's Slide Direct route on Mont Dax, with Louise acting as his guide.

"I already told you, Louise," he replied. "I tried hard to get here in July. But my girlfriend, Marian, was busy then. I couldn't just leave her behind, now could I? You know she wants to climb the mountain too."

"Well, get yourself another guide, then! I'm not the only guide in Montier. There must be a hundred others.

Surely you can find someone who doesn't care about the weather."

"Louise, is it really the weather that's bothering you so much? Is that the real problem?"

"What else? What else could be bothering me?"

Lawrence Darnley, who had said he would arrive by July 10, had been late because his fiancée, Marian Shepherd, needed to attend a wedding back in Montreal. In the many letters that Lawrence had written to Louise, discussing their prospective climb, there had been no mention of anyone else coming along — no mention of a fiancée at all, in fact.

"Louise, try to look at it from her point of view. Marian's a wonderful girl, and she's concerned for my safety. She feels that a three-member party would be less risky, because two people can always get a third off the mountain. It's true, Marian hasn't done as much climbing as you or I. But she's very athletic. She used to study ballet, and last year she competed in the Canadian horseback championships."

"That's very interesting, Lawrence," Louise said coolly. "But as I remember, there aren't any horses up on Mont Dax. It's just rock and ice near the top — and at this time of year, mainly ice. Four weeks ago we might've had a chance. But now it's impossible, simply impossible."

As they continued arguing, Jean-Claude came out on the terrace of the rooming house. He had become re-acquainted with Lawrence the day before, and the two young men had taken a liking to each other. But now Jean-Claude interrupted by saying:

"Lawrence, you have to listen to Louise. She knows

what she's talking about. You can't climb the Devil's Slide this late in the year. And what sort of nonsense is this, to bring an inexpert climber on a route like that? Marian would have a terrible time. Has she ever climbed in a blizzard? And how does she feel about severe exposure — clinging to some evil cliff, with nothing but a thousand yards of empty space under her feet?"

"Marian assures me that she'll do quite well. I've taken her climbing many times, in the Rockies. When we're married, we intend to go everywhere together. Our marriage will be a true partnership, a sharing of deep mutual interests. . . ."

Louise looked away. For some reason, it made her grind her teeth whenever she heard talk of this wonderful impending marriage. Lawrence seemed to be trying to convince himself of something. Over and over, he spoke of the need to "be mature now," to "take on responsibility," "get one's life in order." The four years of medical school had changed him a lot. Before, he had talked of nothing but mountain climbing, having exciting experiences; now, he couldn't wait to return to Montreal, where he had plans for establishing himself in a rich medical practice.

"Marian's father, Brangwen Shepherd, is the finance minister in the government," he explained. "Their family owns twelve lumber mills. Mr. Shepherd has been kind enough to help me buy into the Bernays Clinic, a big medical practice. The patients come from only the finest families in Montreal. . . ."

* * *

That afternoon, while Louise tended to some business at the Guides' Association, Lawrence walked all over Montier, looking for someone to lead him on the Slide. But everyone he spoke to said the same thing. They would be happy to take him up Mont Dax, but not by the Direct route. That evening, as Louise was returning home, she ran into Lawrence on the street. As they were standing together, trying to think of what to say, Marian came out of a nearby shop, where she had been looking for shampoo and conditioner.

"They have only the crudest products here," Marian complained. "Everything's so out of date. With hair like mine" — she had thick, golden hair, which she wore flowing down her back — "ordinary shampoos just won't do. My mother warned me: she said, 'Be sure to stock up when you're in Paris, dear; those little villages where you're going are amusingly primitive.' But I didn't listen to my mother. One *never* listens to one's mother, does one? And then sometimes it turns out that the old dear was right!"

Louise smiled, and she said that she had some good shampoo at home. She would be happy to lend the bottle to Marian.

"Thank you, you're so kind. But your hair is so dark, while mine is . . . extra-fair, wouldn't you say? I don't think the same shampoo could suit us both. Anyway, we're not here to stage a beauty contest. We've come all this way to climb a mountain. Isn't that right, Lawrence? Aren't we going to climb it, right to the top?"

"Yes, that's right, Marian. That's what we came to do."

Lawrence looked extremely glum. Louise felt sad for

him; she knew he had been unable to find another guide, anyone willing to risk the Direct. All his life, Lawrence Darnley had been dreaming of climbing the Devil's Slide. For some reason, this particular route, on this special mountain, meant more to him than anything else.

"Lawrence," Louise said comfortingly, "don't be too unhappy. Maybe we can do it next year. No one else has managed to climb it before — you'll still be able to have the first ascent."

"No, I've missed my chance. I can feel it in my heart. If only we'd gotten here a month ago, as you and I first planned, Louise. Then we really might have made it."

Marian looked nervous as Lawrence spoke these disappointed words. Suddenly covering her eyes with her hands, she burst into tears.

"Oh, Lawrence — I'm so ashamed! I've ruined your whole adventure, haven't I — I've held you back! If only my cousin hadn't had to get married. And Lawrence, you were so sweet about it. I begged you to leave without me, but you wouldn't. You're so unselfish. So good."

"Don't be silly," Lawrence said simply. He put an arm around her shoulders.

Early next morning, Louise left for Chamonix, where she had work as a porter. The weather was bad, with a strong wind blowing from the northeast. Louise was cold the whole time, but the experience put her in an optimistic mood. Her father and other old-time guides had a special name for this kind of wind: they called it *l'ami de poche* (the pocketbook's friend) because, in most years, a spell of good weather came afterward. In the three or four sunny days that followed *l'ami de poche,* a guide could make a lot of money leading late-season climbs.

"Lawrence," she said when she returned, "have you packed up all your equipment? Have you decided not to climb at all this year?"

"Well, since we can't do the Direct, I thought we'd just take some hikes. Marian wants to walk to Lake Belette if the weather ever clears up."

"Yes, it's really foul out there now, isn't it? Just imagine what it's like up on the Direct — why, we'd have frozen to death."

"You were right, Louise, I have to admit it. You were definitely right."

A minute later Louise surprised him by saying, "You know, I think maybe I've changed my mind. I'd like to give it a try now — even in this bad weather. How about it, Lawrence? Are you still eager to climb the Direct?"

Lawrence stared at Louise for a long moment. He assumed, of course, that she was joking.

"Well? Are you still in the mood?" she said. "Because if you are, we should get right to work. We have lots of packing to do. We'll need provisions for three or four days, plus all the equipment. If we get ready tonight, we can be off tomorrow morning."

"But Louise — what in the world are you talking about? The wind's blowing at fifty miles an hour out there. It looks like it's going to snow. We wouldn't have a chance. And besides, Marian has a bad cold — she's in bed upstairs."

"Is Marian still planning to come?"

"Well, I don't know. . . ."

The next morning, just after 4:00 A.M., a small party set out from Montier. In the predawn dark, it was impossible to tell who was who; but the person walking at the head of the line, carrying a big rucksack, was Louise. Behind her came Lawrence Darnley, also carrying a large pack; and behind them came Marian Shepherd and Jean-Claude.

Every few minutes, Marian pulled out a handkerchief and blew her nose loudly. She was feeling miserable, she let them know, but she was determined to "protect" Lawrence by joining him on this climb. The wind that had blown so fiercely for the last several days was dying out now; by the time they reached the old stone bridge, which crossed an icy creek flowing down from the glacier, the air had become quite still.

"Louise!" Lawrence said, amazed. "It's just as you promised! As soon as dawn showed in the sky, the wind stopped completely."

"Yes, and if we're lucky, the next few days will all be calm. That's how it always is after *l'ami de poche.*"

"Oh, Lawrence," Marian complained. "I have a terrible headache. It must be my sinuses — the air up here is so sharp and cold."

"Do you need my handkerchief, Marian? Can I get you some aspirin?"

"No. You know I can't take aspirin. It ruins my stomach."

As the party continued past the stone bridge, Marian

began to cry softly. Jean-Claude, walking behind her, stepped up and supported her over the hardest parts of the trail. She said that she was wearing the wrong sort of shoes — these heavy climbing boots were making her legs tired, and they would surely give her blisters.

"As soon as we get to the little glacier," Louise promised, "we'll take a good break. But we have to keep moving now. We want to be on the wall by nine A.M. sharp. That's the only way we'll have a chance to get to the caves by nightfall."

"Oh, Lawrence — *do* something!" Marian wailed.

Lawrence shook his head. "Louise is in charge, dear. We have to do as she says. Be brave for a while longer, and we'll take a rest at the glacier. Would you like me to hold your hand?"

"No! At least there's *one* gentleman in this party. . . . Jean-Claude, will you come here? Help me over this steep part, please."

Two hours later, at 7:30, they reached the little glacier. Louise led them along the side of it, and soon they were at the bergschrund, the place where the glacier met the base of the mountain wall. A gap had formed where the glacier had melted back from the rock; Louise climbed down into this gap, trailing a rope behind her.

"I can get across," she called up a moment later. "It's very icy down here — everybody better put on his crampons. It'll take me a minute to fix the rope. Then I'll come back up."

When Louise climbed out of the bergschrund, she

found Lawrence and Jean-Claude kneeling in front of Marian. They were taking off her hiking boots. Marian, sitting on a large block of ice, was moaning and grimacing, presumably because her feet hurt.

"No, Lawrence — no!" she cried angrily. "Don't wrench the shoe back and forth. Be more gentle, like Jean-Claude!"

"Yes, dear. . . ."

Eventually, the two men got both her boots off. Louise came over to examine Marian's feet. She found one small blister on the back of Marian's left heel, but nothing serious.

"I have some tape to put on that blister. Maybe you should wear an extra pair of socks, too — that'll give you more protection."

"Oh, *thank* you, Miss DeMaistre! Thank you so much! You're so extraordinarily kind!"

Marian looked hard at Louise; Louise was tempted to say something unpleasant back to her, but she controlled herself. Marian's bare feet, with their little pink toes, looked so silly at that moment — wriggling out in the cold air, there on the ice field — that Louise laughed instead. She went over to her pack to get the tape. She offered Marian one of her own extra pairs of socks.

"I'd rather not take them," Marian said. "You might need them yourself — on your *wonderful, important climb*. The climb must go on — the climb before everything! The brave mountaineers must reach the top, no matter what!"

Again, Louise was tempted to laugh. But when she looked at Lawrence, she could see how uncomfortable he felt, and she suppressed the urge.

"Let's just rest for another few minutes," she said calmly. "Then we'll tackle the bergschrund. We're still pretty much on schedule. We can make good progress if the weather holds."

As Louise was walking away, chewing an apple, she heard Lawrence speak to Marian. She couldn't make out the words, but Marian's response was to burst into tears. "Never . . . if you don't . . . *I mean it!*" Marian said fiercely; after which Lawrence spoke to her quietly for a few more minutes.

Then, as Louise was climbing down into the bergschrund again, Jean-Claude tapped her on the shoulder. With a wink he said:

"I don't think I'll be going farther today, Louise. I think I'll head back to town. By the way — Marian's decided to come back with me. She says her head hurts too much. It's still bothering her."

"I see," Louise said quietly. "Well . . . take care of her, then. See she doesn't hurt herself on the trail. I guess I'll just push on with Lawrence — I'm not sure how far we can go, but we'll give it a try."

"Good luck, Sister. I wish you the best. And take care of yourself."

Thus, only two people began the actual climb that morning on Mont Dax. By 9:30, Louise and Lawrence had crossed the bergschrund and begun on the wall; by about 1:00 P.M., when they broke for a quick lunch, they were two thousand feet above the glacier.

Thirteen

Louise only began to worry when they reached the area below the caves. The afternoon sun had begun to warm the banks of snow high on the Slide; and like clockwork, avalanches began to come down. Every nine or ten minutes another one swept past. The great waves of snow made a hissing, then a rumbling, then a roaring sound as they tumbled by.

"Isn't it magnificent?" cried Lawrence. "There's not another wall like this in the world! Even the Eiger North isn't so deadly, so scary! Just imagine — the Devil's Slide itself!"

Louise could only shake her head and smile. Lawrence had climbed all that morning with a furious energy: his joyful fearlessness made her think of a caged animal suddenly set free. They had covered the first half of the south buttress route in record-setting time. If the weather held, they would be among the caves in another forty-five minutes. Then, if they could avoid the avalanches, they might reach the top before nightfall.

"Louise, let me lead the next pitch," he said. "It's my turn."

"Didn't we say that I would lead when we got to the caves, Lawrence? Wasn't that our agreement?"

"Yes, I know. I'm perfectly willing to admit it, Louise — you're the better climber, especially on snow and ice. But I feel so strong at the moment. I don't think I could stand it, watching you lead all the fun parts."

"Fun? Is that what you call this next pitch, up that brutal crack full of ice? And what about the avalanches, Lawrence? Have you noticed how regular they are?"

"Yes. There seems to be a new one every few minutes."

"Every nine and a quarter minutes, to be exact. I've been timing them with my watch."

"Well, you just stay here, Louise, and go on timing them. Meanwhile, I'll do a little climbing."

Eventually, they decided that Lawrence would lead the next pitch. Louise would watch the time as she belayed; every nine minutes, she would call up, to remind Lawrence that another avalanche was due.

"And when I shout, that means take cover. Hide under an overhang, get inside a cave, do anything. We're not in the direct path of the avalanches, so it shouldn't be too bad. But be careful."

"All right — here I go."

Lawrence, climbing with speed and strength, was soon many yards above. Louise watched as he disappeared around a little corner; then, since nine minutes had elapsed, she called up the icy crack. She heard a faint reply. Precisely on schedule, another avalanche came roaring and hissing down. The bulk of the snowfall passed well to the left of their positions.

"I'm all right!" Lawrence called a moment later. "My, what fun! What a beautiful, terrible mountain this is! How spectacular!"

Louise could hardly hear him after a while. She realized that after another minute he would be completely out of earshot. The route now tended toward the left, into the direct path of the avalanches. The belay line ran through her fingers slowly, as Lawrence, far above, climbed out of the icy crack.

"Lawrence!" she shouted suddenly. "It's time! It's nine minutes, Lawrence. Take cover!"

There was no reply. The belay line kept inching up, which meant that he was still climbing; but if he happened to be in an exposed position when the avalanche arrived, he would be swept off. Then only the belay rope, and Louise's grip on it, could save his life.

"Lawrence!" she screamed. "Lawrence . . . !"

Ten minutes had passed. Then — eleven and a half. Louise kept looking at her watch. She heard a great rumbling far above, a sound much louder than anything they had heard before. The belay line continued to inch up, and then — it suddenly stopped.

Seconds later, a great avalanche swept down. Not only did it make a louder sound, it caused a strong, piercing wind to blow down the mountain face; this wind was actually a wall of air being pushed in front of the snowfall. Louise was almost knocked off her belay stance. The cascade of snow hit her directly, making her lose all sense of where she was. Nor could she catch her breath: the air was so full of snow that it was like being under water.

After minutes of near suffocation, she felt the wind slacken. The pressure of snow and ice against her eased up, and the air started to clear. Slowly, the mountain re-formed itself in her eyes. She could see the rocks directly above her, then the icy crack, which was full of fresh snow. After another minute or two she could see the whole south face: thousands of feet of sheer, ice-covered rock both above and below.

"Lawrence!" she called. "Are you up there? Lawrence . . . !"

There was still no answer. After the roaring, whirling turmoil of the avalanche, the mountain was strangely quiet and peaceful. Louise heard nothing, no human voice or response.

"I'm coming up!" she suddenly cried. "Hold on, Lawrence! I'm coming!"

Thinking that he might still be alive (though buried under yards of snow), she moved as quickly as she could. Soon she was far up the crack; the belay rope, tied around her waist, fell in a loose loop below her. But when she was almost out of the crack, something strange began to happen. The rope began to be pulled up, slowly reeled in from above. By the time she was at the top of the crack, there was hardly any slack left.

When she reached a snow-covered boulder, she made a pleasant discovery. Here was Lawrence, squatting comfortably on his heels, casually pulling in the rope wrapped around her waist.

"What took you so long?" he asked dryly. "I'm beginning to get cold, sitting here in the snow like this."

"I was sure you were finished, Lawrence . . . swept off or buried. Why didn't you answer when I called?"

"I didn't hear you, Louise. Were you calling? Then I looked at my watch, and it seemed like a long time had gone by. And then — the avalanche came."

He had hidden under the boulder, he said. But he almost suffocated down there. The space under the rock kept filling up with snow, and he had to kick it clear several times. When the snow finally stopped rushing past, he dug his way out. Feeling movement on the end of the line, he began to reel it in, as Louise climbed up from below.

"Lawrence — that was a *very* big avalanche," she now exclaimed. "The biggest I've ever seen. We can't count on only little ones anymore; if there's an interval of more than ten minutes, it means that a much larger one is coming down. Then we've really got to watch out."

"I don't know about all this climbing-by-the-watch business," he answered calmly. "You've just got to take your chances, it seems to me. If an avalanche hits when you're exposed, that's just too bad. There's nothing to do about it."

Louise replied, "I agree, there's nothing you can do. But *before* that point, if you count the intervals carefully, you just may save your life. You have to pay attention up here,

Lawrence. Everything that happens on the peaks has some meaning. Anyhow, let's start moving again. There's bound to be a long interval before the next one. Now's our chance to make some progress."

Two hours later, with Louise leading on the rope, they climbed completely clear of the caves. Now they were higher up on the Devil's Slide than any climbers had ever been before in history. The sun had gone down — there was still enough light to climb by, but Louise knew that in another hour it would turn dark.

"I think I'll lead this next pitch," she said to Lawrence. "I still feel strong. And I'm more confident on snow than you are."

"All right, Louise — whatever you say."

Stretching ahead of them — and looking like nothing very special, just a long, windy patch of snow — was the famous Devil's Slide itself. Seen from several miles below, down in the valley of Montier, the Slide resembled the white mark on a horse's forehead. It was shaped like a diamond, and the bottom part — the place where Louise and Lawrence were standing at this moment — came to a definite point. What made the Slide different from other snowfields, however, was the steep angle at which it lay. Louise could hardly believe that the entire mass didn't break free, just come crashing down on them.

"It's a little scary," she heard herself say. "A bit unstable looking. But we've come this far, haven't we, Lawrence? We might as well give it a try."

"That's right. And by the way — stay over to the left, Louise. The snow on that side looks more solid."

Soon Louise had crossed onto the snowfield itself. Lawrence, holding the end of the rope, remained below her on the point. With each step, Louise sank into the snow up to her thighs; she had nothing to grab with her hands, and sometimes she made progress only by lying flat on the surface, stretching her arms and legs out, and "swimming" upward. But after a while, she felt a layer of firmer snow beneath the surface. Now when her boots sank down they encountered this harder level, and she began to move more quickly.

There had been no avalanches for the last thirty minutes. She stopped timing the intervals; now that the sun was down, the snowfield was beginning to freeze again, and this made it safer to cross. But sometimes, when she stepped through to the hard-packed level, the mountain seemed to tremble under her feet. This was an unpleasant sensation: it meant that the hard layer, rather than being firmly attached, was itself only floating on another, deeper, softer level.

Arriving at a suitable belay stance, she gave three tugs on the rope. This was the signal they had arranged together: it meant that Lawrence could begin climbing now. (In conditions of extreme avalanche danger, climbers never shout up and down a slope to one another; the vibrations of the human voice can cause an avalanche to break free.) The wind had stopped completely, and from out of nowhere a flock of little birds appeared. They were the quick, gray-backed Alpine sparrows known as *coeurs des aigles* (hearts of eagles). These tiny birds are respected for their complete lack of fear on the high slopes, and they live only in the windiest, coldest passes in the mountains. While Lawrence was climbing up, Louise watched the birds fly back and forth across the snowfield. Sometimes they only skimmed the surface, but occasionally, they actually landed in the snow.

"I wonder why they do that," she mused. "Now they seem to be pecking at the snow — could it be that there's something to eat in it? Insects, or seeds? And now they've all taken off again — they're just hovering over the snow, like a bunch of gray hummingbirds."

Only an instant later, Louise felt the sickening movement in the snow again. The section of the field where she was standing seemed to tilt — it was like standing on a steep, slippery roof and feeling the shingles start to slide. But then the feeling passed.

"Thank God," she said to herself. "Thank God. And look — the birds have landed again. They must know when it's safe to be on the snow, and when it isn't. If only Lawrence would hurry. We have to get off this horrible snowfield. Oh, please," she prayed, "please let him hurry. . . ."

Just as he was coming into view, the birds took off again. But this time, they didn't hover over the surface; they flew quickly up into the air, as if afraid to be anywhere near the snow surface. Louise had only a second to tighten her grip on the rope. She managed to shout a single word — "Avalanche!" — before the whole mountain seemed to come loose under her feet.

Fourteen

"It happens sometimes in the mountains that you live . . . or you don't. All you can do is pray."

These words, once spoken by her father, echoed in Louise's ears. The first thing she felt was a crushing pain. The belay line was cutting into her flesh; she was dangling free in space, and the ledge she had been standing on, which she had chopped out with her ice ax, had entirely disappeared.

"I must get back to the wall," she said. "I must . . ."

She grabbed hold of a piece of ice. But when she pulled toward the wall, the piece broke off. Her ice ax was still attached to her wrist, dangling by a leather thong. She took the ax and slammed it into the wall; the head of the ax bit, and she pulled herself closer.

"Now . . . if only I could turn my body. But the belay line's cutting me in half. Can't do it . . ."

Something stirred on the other end of the rope. Lawrence's body, tied to the other end, was twisting in the wind. As it did, Louise also twisted to her right. Soon she was almost facing the wall.

"Good. Much better," she said, trying to encourage herself. But the weight of Lawrence's body was terrible; she knew she could hold it for only a few more seconds. The belay rope was simply choking the life out of her.

"I must . . . kick myself into the wall. Kick my crampons into the wall." With a great effort, she began to chip at the ice with her feet. She cut out two shallow holes, which would serve her as steps. Pulling herself against the wall, she stood up in these little steps.

"There. That's very good," she said aloud. "Now I'm not being pulled in two directions. Only . . . from below. . . ."

The pressure of Lawrence's body was tremendous. It was like having a heavy sack of sand tied tightly to your waist. Louise was certain that Lawrence was dead: the avalanche had broken off just under her feet, then the full force of it had fallen on top of him. Only by a cruel miracle was his body still attached to the rope. This meant that she, too, was going to have to die.

"Oh, Lawrence," she said softly, "if only I were stronger. If I were my father, I could pull your body straight up; then I could take you off the rope. But I'm not strong enough . . . soon I won't be able to breathe anymore."

She had only one hope. In a back pocket of her rucksack she carried a small knife. If she could get her hands on this, she could cut the rope. Then Lawrence's body would fall free, and she might survive.

With the last bit of her strength, she groped for the knife. But the pocket where she always kept it was on the wrong side of her pack — the side she couldn't reach with her free hand. No matter how she twisted and bent, she couldn't quite get to it.

"Oh, well," she said, "it doesn't matter, anyway. I guess we'll die together, Lawrence. Everything's going dark now. The whole world's going dark. . . ."

As she lost consciousness, Louise leaned out from the ice wall. She relaxed her grip on her ax, and her feet began to slip out of the shallow steps. But now something remarkable happened. The weight of Lawrence's body, the pressure which was squeezing the life out of her, suddenly lessened. Responding to this new feeling on the rope, Louise pulled herself close to the wall again. Then she stood up straight in the shallow steps. A few seconds later she was breathing almost normally.

"Lawrence . . . Lawrence," she murmured.

There was a definite stirring on the rope. The line hung down from her more slackly, less directly; a moment later, she saw movement below her.

"Lawrence! Lawrence!" she cried.

And there came this answer: "I'm coming up, Louise. I'm coming up! What a terrible headache I've got — half the mountain fell on my neck. . . ."

As Louise watched, Lawrence, the "dead man," climbed slowly toward her. Soon he was just below her position. She reached down, helping him up the last few feet.

Fifteen

When the avalanche hit, Lawrence had been standing close to the ice wall. Pressing his body even closer, he assumed a position that allowed most of the snow to pass over him, to roll off his back harmlessly.

"Still — it was awful," he said. "I was sure I was finished. One chunk of ice smashed right on my head, and I must have lost consciousness. The next thing I knew, I was dangling on the end of the rope. I looked up and saw you chipping steps in the ice. If you hadn't been strong enough to hold me, Louise, we both would've been goners."

"Lawrence, I almost cut you off the rope. I just couldn't reach my pocketknife — that's all that saved you, Lawrence."

He looked at her sharply for a moment. Then he laughed heartily.

"No, Lawrence — I mean it, I'm telling you the truth. I tried to cut you off, I tried to get your body off the rope."

"Oh, I believe you, Louise. I really do. It's just that . . . it seems funny, somehow. Like a big joke."

"A big . . . joke?"

"Yes. A crazy joke that the mountain is playing on us. It's as if someone was toying with us, showing us how completely helpless we are up here. And then — letting us live, for some strange reason."

The night that followed — ten hours of darkness and freezing temperatures — was possibly the hardest part of the whole experience. Unable to move farther up in the dark, they stayed on the tiny steps that Louise had cut. The temperature fell to ten degrees Fahrenheit, and strong winds nearly blew them off their perch.

"Louise, are you still alive?" Lawrence asked at one point. "Can you still feel your hands and feet?"

"Yes, I think I can. What about you — does your head still hurt? Is your neck sore?"

"Th-that's the good thing about being so cold," he replied through clenched teeth. "It makes you forget all about your other problems."

Shaking and groaning from the cold, they remained huddled together, afraid to sit or lie down. If they had dozed off, they would have frozen to death. They knew that in the mountains, in such conditions, death comes quickly for those who relax.

"You know, Louise, I still can't believe I'm alive," Lawrence whispered in the dark. "I don't even care about the cold so much — it just reminds me that we're still here. That we've survived."

"It's a little early to say we've survived, don't you think, Lawrence? There's a long time till morning. Then we have another three hundred yards to climb. Straight up the vertical ice."

"Oh, we'll make it," he replied. "I'm sure of that now. The two of us together can't be defeated — don't you feel that? Don't you know that in your bones?"

Louise thought she knew what he meant. She had a certain feeling of irrational confidence when she climbed with Lawrence; it was a feeling of invincibility, as if nothing in the world could ever stop them. "Well," she said offhandedly, "maybe you're right, Lawrence, maybe not. But I sure wish you'd stop shivering so much — you're about to shake us off this ledge."

At half past five that morning, the sky started to lighten, and they began to climb again. The upper half of the Devil's Slide had frozen solid during the night, and the going was easier — and safer — now. Soon the summit ridge came into view. At about ten o'clock, they stood together on the very peak of Mont Dax. It was the second of September 1956. Lawrence, in his enthusiasm, threw his arms around Louise; as he kissed her, he lifted her right off her feet.

Back in Montier, several friends awaited their return. Jean-Claude greeted them at the rooming house, and after embracing them he warned them that many reporters would be arriving that evening. Word had already gotten out that they had succeeded — that two climbers had actually completed the terrible Devil's Slide Direct, which had claimed so many lives.

"And was it really so terrible?" her brother asked. "What was it really like, to stand on that huge, unstable field of snow?"

"It was . . . interesting," Louise said. "Very interesting. I'd like to do it again someday. Maybe we could all go up together next time — make a regular picnic out of it."

"A picnic?" inquired Hervet, Louise's young guiding friend. "I know exactly what kind of picnic it was. I was watching you all day yesterday, through the telescope out on the balcony. Just as it got dark I saw a huge avalanche come down from the Slide. It must have fallen right on top of you."

"No, not on top of me," Louise said dryly. "On top of Lawrence. Ask him about it — he's the one who nearly lost his head."

Lawrence, with a sudden look of exaggerated pain, groaned and rubbed the back of his neck, remembering the massive icefall.

A few minutes later, as Lawrence was heading upstairs, Jean-Claude took him aside and handed him a letter. The envelope was pink and smelled of perfume. Lawrence tore it open quickly, and as he read the note, his expression became rather serious.

"Lawrence — what is it? Bad news?" Louise wondered.

"Well . . . yes, I'm afraid. It is bad news. But not . . . unexpected." Then he explained: "It's Marian. She's left me, it seems. She's gone back to Paris. She says she realized that . . . well, that we could never be happy together. Could never make a life together. When I decided to continue climbing, it became clear to her how selfish I really am, that I only think about my own success. And you know — she's right. When I saw that you and I had a chance to make it, I forgot all about Marian, I forgot about everything. All I cared about, from that moment on, was getting to the top of that mountain."

"But Lawrence — that's perfectly natural," Louise replied. "That's exactly what it means to be a climber. You have to be single-minded. You have to have a great drive to succeed, or you won't get anywhere. Everybody knows that."

"Yes, I know it, too. But it's not something I feel very good about right now. Poor Marian — she was so disappointed, so surprised at how I acted. She always thought that we would do everything together . . . then, at the first opportunity, I left her behind."

Sixteen

The next morning, Louise and Lawrence held a press conference. Many newspaper reporters crowded into the parlor of the DeMaistres' rooming house, and they asked the two young climbers countless questions about their adventure. What had conditions really been like on the mountain? What exactly was the route they took — was it the classic route first described by Alex DeGrazi in his book? And how bad were the avalanches, really? Et cetera, et cetera. Jules DeMaistre stood in a corner of the room, puffing on his pipe and looking proudly at his daughter every now and again. When one of the reporters directed a question his way, he calmly refused to answer. "No, you'll have to ask Louise about that," he said. "She knows more about it than I do."

Louise was embarrassed by all the attention, but she also enjoyed it. Hearing herself described as a "heroine of

French climbing," as "the great Louise, princess of the Alps," was a lot of fun, to tell the truth. Even so, she remembered clearly how it had been just the day before: how it had felt almost to freeze to death, to cling to their tiny, icy perch for ten hours.

"If I'm such a heroine," she whispered to Lawrence, "then why was I so scared yesterday? Why was I shivering with fear, almost too afraid to take a breath?"

"But you *are* a heroine," Lawrence whispered back. "These people are right. You did what no one else could, Louise. And face it: without you, I never would've reached the top. You took all the hard leads."

"No, Lawrence, don't you remember the icy crack? You were magnificent there. And it took real courage to stand under the point of the snowfield while I climbed above you. You knew if I set off an avalanche it would fall right on your head."

"Excuse me, Dr. Darnley," interrupted one of the reporters. "May I ask you a personal question?"

"Why, yes, certainly. Go right ahead."

"Since you've achieved your great goal, are there any other challenges for you here in the Alps? Many people believe that the Devil's Slide was the last classic route remaining to be climbed in Europe. Will you return to Canada now? Or have you some other destination?"

"Well," Lawrence said uncertainly, "I don't really know. I'll return to Canada eventually, but I'm not ready to give up climbing yet. The most exciting routes in the world are in Asia now, in Nepal and Tibet: the northwest ridge of

Mount Everest, for example, or the south face of Annapurna. These are the challenges that a modern climber dreams about. Of course, I have no experience in that part of the world. Maybe I'm only fooling myself, but I'd like to climb one of the eight-thousand-meter peaks someday. Mount Changamal would be a good one. That's the one they call the Blue Lioness, because of its terrible, icy northwest face. If I'm not mistaken, a German party recently met defeat there. Several people died, as I recall. . . ."

This press conference, which was supposed to last only an hour, ran well into the afternoon. When it was over, Louise went straight upstairs; she was still exhausted from the day before, and she slept straight through till morning, sixteen hours all told.

The next morning, there occurred this conversation:

"But where *is* he, Jean-Claude? His room is empty."

"I know, Louise. Don't take it personally, but he had important business. Something he had to attend to in Paris."

Louise had awakened to find Lawrence gone. He hadn't even left her a note. "He said to offer you his apologies," Jean-Claude continued, "and to say he'll be back sometime. But he had to see someone in Paris."

Louise knew very well who this someone was. His fiancée, of course, Marian Shepherd. Undoubtedly, Lawrence had run off to beg for another chance, to ask her not to leave him. Just the idea of this made Louise terribly angry. Didn't he have any pride; was he really so foolish as to chase after such a girl? Anyone could see that Marian, and not Lawrence, was the truly selfish one. She thought of nothing but her own comfort and satisfaction. She had opposed the climb of the Devil's Slide from the beginning; she had done everything she could to sabotage the effort, first by postponing the start of it, then by all her complaining, her various "headaches," "sore feet," and so on.

Lawrence, the bold, courageous climber, was another man entirely back on the ground. On the cliffs he was strong and decisive, but he became weak in the clutches of someone like Marian, who could twist him any way she wanted. There had been moments on their recent climb together when Louise had felt something very special for Lawrence; for example, when he said that he thought the two of them could never be defeated. At that moment, she had believed that there was indeed a special bond between them, and that his feelings for her were . . . more than just friendly.

Now, in addition to being angry with him, she felt deeply embarrassed for herself. She had been fooling herself for years, secretly hoping that Lawrence would one day think of her as more than just a climbing partner. She could remember dozens of times when this hope of hers had been painfully obvious; when Lawrence, chuckling to himself all the while, must have thought, "Ah, the little fool — she just adores me. Well, I'll try not to hurt her feelings too badly. Maybe it's even best to encourage her fantasy; that way, she'll always be willing to climb with me, which is all I really want from her."

Thinking about it this way — imagining that Lawrence had actually been laughing at her — Louise felt depressed. Two days later, when she had still not heard a word from him, she caught a cold from being out in a freezing rain. This cold soon turned into the flu, which then turned into a case of pneumonia.

Seventeen

"No, Hervet. I don't feel like climbing. I'm still much too weak."

It was the spring of 1957. Louise had been sick all winter. Hervet, her good friend, had come to visit her at home.

"But the season's beginning, Louise. The southern slopes are free of ice now," he said. "In another few weeks, the clients will start to arrive. Many are asking to climb with you. You have a reputation now, you know."

Although Louise was over being sick, the prospect of climbing excited her not at all. She preferred staying home all the time, reading novels and dozing in her upstairs bedroom. Some friends of hers, thinking to shake her out of the doldrums, asked her to come on a difficult ice climb with them in the massif. But she refused.

"You don't need me, Hervet, I'd only slow you down,"

she said. "I have an unlucky feeling these days. Nothing interests me very much. Did you ever get the feeling that nothing really matters, that the world just goes on and on, and no one ever gets anywhere? What difference does it make if I climb a frozen gully somewhere on the Dent du Géant? Does that make life any better — does it even make it bearable?"

Some of her friends, hearing Louise talk this way, decided that the great victory on the Devil's Slide had gone to her head. Apparently, she considered herself too important to go on simple climbs anymore. These friends now avoided her. But Hervet knew that something else was the matter, and he refused to leave her alone.

"All right, don't come then, Louise — but there's only one cure for how you feel. You have to wake up, you have to challenge yourself! Come climbing with me next Saturday. When you're out there risking your neck, it's funny how interesting things become."

Almost against her will, Louise prepared for the climb on Saturday. Her ice- and rock-climbing equipment looked strange to her, as if it belonged to someone else. Knowing that Hervet proposed to challenge her, she forced herself to go on a few hard walks that week. Her lungs had gotten much weaker: simply hiking up from the village to the first glacier, a distance of about four miles, left her gasping for breath. But after five days of hikes she felt some of her old stamina returning. Still, it was one thing to hike on gently rising ground, quite another to climb on vertical rock and ice. On Saturday, she confessed her fears to Hervet.

"You don't understand — I have no strength left. Just look at my arms, Hervet. They're like two sticks."

"You won't need muscles, not at all, Louise. Just come along. We'll ride the *téléférique* up to the col, then climb a few pitches. Nothing too hard."

"All right. But don't expect miracles."

The morning was very cold, a last taste of winter. At nine o'clock, when they reached the col (a high mountain pass), cold sunlight suddenly streamed over the eastern peaks. Here in the lower reaches of the massif, the air was extremely fresh, with a slight flavor of water and iron. Louise trudged along behind Hervet with her head down. Though her pack weighed only about thirty pounds, her neck and shoulders soon felt sore, and she was grateful each time Hervet called a rest.

"Look at that view, Louise; isn't it wonderful? Ah, the Alps," he said. "Europe's playground."

"I'm not some tourist, Hervet," she answered dryly. "I've been up here a few times before, remember? Save the pretty speeches for the ladies you guide on Sunday."

Hervet smiled. "But you look so grim. I just want you to enjoy yourself, Louise."

"When I've begun enjoying myself, I'll let you know."

Soon they reached a wall without a special name. Here they removed their packs and roped up, Hervet taking the lead. Louise followed him up an easy pitch, after which they tackled something slightly harder. Louise was relieved to find that everything worked almost as before; she was much weaker, but her sense of balance was good, and she climbed by relying more on this, less on brute strength and speed. However, something was troubling her. She had a strange sense of being only half awake, of not being really "present" on the cliff. It was as if she were watching herself from a distance, coldly evaluating every move she made. When they reached the end of the second pitch, Hervet asked if she wanted to continue, to tackle something harder. To his surprise she burst into tears.

"But — what is it? What's the matter?"

"It's just . . . it's no good, Hervet, that's all. It's just not the same for me. I feel so strange — as if I don't belong. I realize now what I've been so afraid of: that I would climb and not really care about it anymore. That it would be dead for me. It's no use, Hervet . . . I'm finished."

They both fell silent. Hervet didn't know what to do or say. Louise wiped her eyes after a while, and she sat down behind a large flake of granite. A moment later, she began to laugh at herself.

"But I'm so ridiculous. What am I crying for, what really? The great Louise DeMaistre doesn't like the mountains anymore. Well, so what? What's the big tragedy? I don't like *anything* anymore. I'm just no use to anybody — not even myself."

"Don't talk that way, Louise. I have to agree with you — you *are* ridiculous. A long time has passed, and you've had some hard experiences. That's all. You have to take things slowly, gradually. This is just the first day out. I don't feel the same, either . . . when we were roping up, I kept thinking about old Bruzel. Do you remember that silly old fool, how he almost broke your leg for you? I kept thinking about what he said one day: 'Pretty girls don't belong in the mountains; they should be down in the valley, larking about in some meadow.' Do you remember that?"

"Yes, I remember. But . . . so what?"

"Oh, it's just that . . . until he said that, I think I hadn't realized that you *are* a girl. No — I'm serious! I thought of you as just another climber, an apprentice guide. Someone good to have on the rope, but not someone who was . . . quite pretty, in fact."

Louise looked quickly at Hervet. She could tell from the sound of his voice that he was embarrassed — he hadn't meant to say something so personal. But they were such old, good friends; surely it was a mistake to let things change between them. The last thing she wanted was for romance — that scary, painful set of feelings — to intervene.

"Thank you, Hervet. I appreciate what you told me. And yes — I really *am* a girl," she assured him. "Sometimes I wonder if that doesn't mean that I'm weak — weak here, in my heart. I feel things too strongly sometimes. This winter, I had a kind of suffering that I don't ever want to have again. I don't think I could stand it."

"Louise, if you feel things too strongly, it isn't because you're a girl. And believe me, there's nothing wrong with your heart! Anyone who can climb the Slide has nothing wrong with her, inside or out. Things just don't work out sometimes. The people we like may not feel the same way toward us . . . that's just how it is. We have to accept it."

"Yes, I know you're right. But it's hard."

This bit of good advice — to accept what can't be changed in life — suddenly struck her as enormously funny. Or maybe it wasn't what Hervet had said, but the simple fact that it was he who said it: Hervet, who was only two months older than she (not even twenty yet); Hervet, with his simple blue eyes, pink cheeks, and eternally uncombed mop of straw-colored hair.

"Hervet — I didn't know you were so wise. Thanks for the philosophy. But seriously: I have to stop moping, I know it. Let's have another climb then, shall we? What about that *dièdre* over there, the one with snow still on it? I think it's my turn to take the lead. . . ."

After a moment, Hervet also smiled. There was a look in Louise's eyes, a certain expression that he remembered from long ago: this wasn't the way someone looked when she had given up, when she was feeling defeated. "All right," he said agreeably, "you take the lead. But that corner looks like trouble. Do you really think we can do it?"

"Come on, Hervet — don't be timid. Everyone needs a little challenge now and again. . . ."

Eighteen

Louise had received a letter from Lawrence Darnley. He had written her in November of 1956, only two months after the Slide. But his letter was very impersonal, all about mountaineering and related subjects; there was hardly a word about himself, or about Marian, or about his plans for the future. About his abrupt departure for Paris, he had only this to say:

"I hope you'll forgive me. I had a lot on my mind . . . when I woke up that morning, I knew I had to get to Paris immediately; duty required it. To stay in Montier would have been wrong, a waste of time, you might say. . . ."

"A waste of time" — so *this* was how he thought about the days he had spent with her. Reading Lawrence's letter made Louise feel even more unhappy, and she decided not to write him back. Nor did she reply to the three other letters he wrote in the next few months. On the day she went climbing with Hervet, in fact, she had just received a fourth letter; but rather than cause herself more pain, she put it away unread.

Still feeling weak, but determined to get on with things, to resume her normal life, she went to work for the Guides' Association again. As Hervet had said, a number of clients were requesting her as their guide; apparently, they wanted to climb with the "famous female mountaineer," and Louise had bookings every week. Since she had worked as a porter for more than three years, she was eligible now to apply for her *carnet,* the official certificate of a full-fledged guide. The application process was very complicated: first, she had to pass two written exams; then, she had to take a practical test, involving difficult climbing; finally, she needed to submit a list of her mountaineering accomplishments to the board of the Association. If everything went well, she would be granted the *carnet* in August, just before her twentieth birthday.

"In which case, I'll be the youngest guide in the history of the Association. As well as the first girl," she bragged to her brother, Jean-Claude.

"Really, Louise, your vanity knows no limits. I guess you expect another bunch of magazine articles. With lots of color photos."

"I'm doing this for one reason only, Jean-Claude: to beat your own record. You won your *carnet* last year, at the age of twenty. That's quite remarkable — for a boy. But I can do better, of course."

Jean-Claude, now a grown man, had already earned a

solid reputation as a guide. His need to assert himself, to prove his courage to everyone he met, had diminished, but he was still a bold climber with an impressive list of first ascents. He was very proud of his younger sister, and if anyone outside the family said a word against her he leapt to her defense. But sometimes her success bothered him; and if she poked fun at his own accomplishments, he could become quite sensitive.

"Yes, you'll do better than I did, Louise. Everyone knows what a *wonder* you are. I've heard people say that climbing with you is like climbing with a machine — Louise never tires, and she never makes a single mistake. But neither does she ever show real friendship, or joy, or excitement. For her the mountains are just a rocky stage — one on which she always proves she's better than everyone else."

After a moment of surprise, Louise replied, "Is that what they say? Is that what people think about me? But what about you, Jean-Claude: is that how you feel, too? Has it always been such a cold, unpleasant experience climbing with me?"

"Think who your friends are, Louise. You have Hervet, who follows you around like a devoted puppy; but the others are all nervous with you, almost afraid. They don't understand what drives you on. Is it love of the mountains? Is it the desire for fame and fortune? If you only wanted to be rich, to be known all over the world, they could understand you better, I think. But nothing seems to satisfy you. Nothing really makes you happy."

"Don't tell me what makes me happy, please — I'll be

the judge of that. And if people feel they don't understand me, well, that's just too bad. I climb for the same reasons as anyone else. Yes, it's true, I haven't been so happy these days; but if you cared about me, if you were sensitive to my feelings, you would've asked me about it."

"I know you haven't been happy. But I'm talking about something more important, Louise. A person doesn't go into the mountains just to prove his skill. A real climber also values the comradeship, the joy of being with good, loyal companions. . . ."

"These loyal companions you talk about — I think I know who they are. They're the same ones who say bad things about me, who resent my success. If I was to climb on their level, they'd be much happier. But I won't do that for them — and not for you, either. . . ."

Several weeks later, in July, Louise ran into her brother again. That day she was taking her climbing exam: she had to lead a difficult pitch on The Ogre, a peak in the Dauphiné Alps. Jean-Claude had been guiding far from Montier most of the summer. Today, he was leading a group up the same wall Louise was climbing, but by an easier route. They greeted each other stiffly; the truth was, they had never really settled their argument from the other day.

"Hello, I see you're climbing with Tairraz," Jean-Claude said. "He's a hard examiner, as I recall."

Basil Tairraz, a well-known senior guide, was the chief examiner that year; so far, he had shaken his head in disappointment at everything Louise had done.

"Yes, I know he doesn't like me," she answered. "Down

on the glacier he complained about my ice-climbing technique, and up here he says that I lack good form. He keeps making me climb big overhangs. I think he's trying to prove that I don't have enough strength, that I'm not as good as a man."

Hearing this comment, Tairraz — a short, thick-chested man with a beard that came to a point — hurried over. Placing a hand casually on Jean-Claude's elbow, he said:

"My boy, you come from a talented family. The name DeMaistre is like gold in these mountains — everyone depends on it. But we have to protect your reputation. What would people think if someone with that name won the *carnet,* but without having all the necessary skills? When you took your exam, Jean-Claude, we were especially strict with you, if you remember. We knew what the public would expect from a DeMaistre."

Louise's cheeks turned red. She was embarrassed not because of what Tairraz said, but because he had overheard her complaining. Jean-Claude noticed her discomfort, and he replied:

"Yes, Tairraz — I appreciate your concern. But can you really doubt Louise's qualifications? She's one of the three or four best climbers in France these days. In fact, now that Hélène de Fresnay has retired, she's probably the best woman climber in the world."

"Oh, d'you really think so?" answered Tairraz, obviously not impressed. "But I have to point out that Mademoiselle de Fresnay was never certified as a guide. She made some famous first ascents, she pioneered a few good routes, but she never had to bring a party down off a mountain in a blizzard. She never had to go out on rescues in the middle of the night. The skills required of a climber are many, but a guide must be willing to sacrifice himself for others. This takes great courage, and, in the end, generosity of spirit. The world-famous climbers you speak of, these great conquerors of the snowy peaks, are usually cold, selfish people. Not the sort who make good guides, not at all."

Louise hung her head. There was nothing she could say, no way to defend herself. If this was what Tairraz, a respected official, really thought of her, then it was hopeless: no matter how well she climbed, how devoted she was to her duties, they would always think the worst of her.

After a moment Jean-Claude cleared his throat and said, "I understand your point, but I must disagree with you, Tairraz. I know you have many more years of experience than I do, but in one way I'm wiser than you. All my life I've lived with two people who are just such as you describe — two of these famous 'conquerors of the snowy peaks.' My father, of course, and now my sister. Though it was very painful, I had to recognize some years ago that I'd never be able to climb on their level. Failing that, I tried to believe that there was something lacking in them — that my father, for instance, was too strict, and that my sister was just as you say, a little cold and selfish. But you know — I was fooling myself.

"My father was strict, yes; but always for a good purpose. And Louise, from the days when we first climbed Henry's Hat together, has understood much better than I the real purpose of mountaineering. She values comradeship above all else; she's the most generous person I've ever climbed with, the least concerned about her own glory. If her feelings don't always show, that's just because they're unusually deep. And if I should ever be in danger — if I should have an accident out on the rocks someday — there's no one else I want on the rope with me."

Tairraz, a little surprised by this strong, unexpected statement, now cleared his own throat. He looked at Louise; her head was still bowed, and it seemed to him that she was having trouble controlling her emotions. Pulling at the point of his beard he said:

"That's an interesting opinion, Jean-Claude, very interesting. But of course, you're the young lady's brother. We can expect you to think highly of her. But I must apply a more objective test. Louise, if you will, please tie on to the rope now. I want you to climb this first pitch as fast as possible. Pay great attention to your form, and let me see none of the carelessness you showed down below. Remember: I'm climbing right behind you, and a senior guide notices *everything*. . . ."

To her surprise, Louise learned two weeks later that she had passed her examinations. This made her the first woman, as well as the youngest person, ever to be named an official guide in that part of the Alps. At a graduation ceremony held in a tavern in Montier, Basil Tairraz himself handed her the mountain guide's insignia, which she would wear thereafter on her sweater; and Tairraz was later heard to comment that she was one of the strongest candidates he had ever tested.

Nineteen

Two years passed. In the mountains, one season flows swiftly into the next: skiing follows climbing, ice climbing follows skiing, and another summer soon arrives. Louise hardly had any time to rest or reflect, and yet these two years were full of important changes for her. Her brother, Jean-Claude, married a girl from the nearby village of Alby, someone he had known a long time. They went to live in his wife's parents' house, thirty miles south of Montier. Then Hervet, Louise's closest friend, who had failed in his examinations for the *carnet,* announced that he was moving to Grenoble to study dentistry. In vain did Louise point out that he could take the exams again next year, and that he was sure to pass the second time around.

"No, I don't think so," Hervet said sadly. "Anyway, I'm not sure I really want to be a guide. I love the mountains, but a mountaineer's life is hard. And sometimes — very short. I'm an only child, Louise. If something was to happen to me, my mother would have no one left."

"But Hervet, can you really be happy living in Grenoble? And what about all the climbs we planned? What about our new route on the Sabatier Wall, for example?"

"Oh, Louise — you'll find someone else. I'm not the best partner you could get, anyway. What about Luc Edouin? He's very strong, and I know he'd like to climb with you."

"No, Hervet. That one belongs to you and me alone. Maybe next summer. When you come back for a visit."

In December 1959, Jules DeMaistre, who was now sixty-one years old, made an important public announcement. The French Alpine Club, headquartered in Paris, had asked him to lead an all-French expedition into the Himalayas, where they would try to climb Mount Dhaulagiri (26,795 feet). Jules announced that he had only two requirements: first, that he be allowed to pick the members of the group himself; and second, that he play only a minor, supporting role in the actual climbing on the mountain. The Alpine Club agreed to these two conditions, and the newspapers and magazines were soon full of stories about the great national expedition.

A climb in the Himalayas is an extremely complicated venture; sometimes it takes several years of planning and preparation. If a climb in the Alps is like a dance, with two people moving nimbly up the rock, a climb in the Himalayas is like a crowd scene in a movie, with every movement of every person carefully, painstakingly coordinated. Dhaulagiri could be reached only after several weeks of travel, by sea, air, on horseback, and on foot. Tons of equipment had to be gathered, carefully packed, and shipped from France to India, then on from India to Nepal; for the last two hundred miles, all of it would be carried up narrow trails on the backs of porters. Fortunately, the Alpine Club had already raised all the money needed to buy the equipment, and the government of Nepal had granted official permission for the climb. If everything worked according to schedule, the party would set out in March of 1960, with the goal of reaching the summit early in May.

Louise had known about the planned expedition for almost a year. Every climber in France had been talking about nothing else — and those, like Louise, who were well known, who had reputations as strong mountaineers, all hoped to be asked to come along. But the news that her father would lead the expedition took Louise by surprise. He hadn't said a word to her about it; and indeed, she only learned of it by reading about it in the newspapers.

"But, Louise — this is good for you, very good," said Tricoussan, the young guide. "If it was my father who was choosing the team, I might also have a chance of being asked."

"No, Tricoussan, you don't understand. In the first place, the expedition would never ask me, because I'm a woman. Even Hélène de Fresnay never got to climb in the Himalayas, because people thought that having a female on an expedition would be 'disruptive.' And in the second place, my father can't choose either me or Jean-Claude. He might be accused of favoritism then."

"Oh, as for that, I wouldn't worry too much: fathers always help their children get ahead. Everyone says that you and Luc Edouin have the best chance of going from Montier. The rest of the climbers will certainly come from Chamonix."

"Yes, probably they'll all come from Chamonix, as in the past. . . ."

When the list was finally published, in the *Journal de la piste* (a French climbing and camping magazine), Luc Edouin was indeed among the climbers named. But not Louise. She immediately went and congratulated Edouin, and she smiled and joked when people offered her their sympathy; but deep in her heart, she was bitterly disappointed. However, her father's behavior somehow encouraged her. He still hadn't said a word to her about the trip, which was strange; and one night, as the family was sitting down to eat dinner, he calmly remarked to his wife:

"You know, it's sad — Jean-Claude really wanted to come. But his wife made him stay home. Now that the baby's coming, he has to work and earn money."

"Yes, it's too bad," answered Martine DeMaistre. "He so much wanted to be part of your expedition. But he has to learn what it means to be a father. There are expenses — and then there are expenses."

Louise ate her soup. Although this was astonishing news (that Jean-Claude had been asked to go), not for the world would she have cried out, angrily accused her father of being unfair. Somehow, she felt that the final word had not yet been said about who would go to Nepal.

"Oh, and by the way," DeMaistre remarked to his wife, "I'll be going to Paris next week. All the climbers have to take physical exams. Everyone has to be fit and equal to the challenge."

"And you — will you also have to take this exam?"

"Of course. And afterward, everyone will know what a broken-down old wreck I really am. . . ."

Two weeks later, another article appeared in the *Journal de la piste.* One of Jules DeMaistre's team members, a guide named Marc Cassel, had been discovered to suffer from a rare heart ailment, one which might cause him trouble at altitudes above twenty thousand feet. Regretfully, Cassel resigned from the team.

"I hear they've already replaced him," Tricoussan said to Louise. "And you know, politics requires them to choose another man from Chamonix. Your poor father has had to fight over every choice; the French Alpine Club, which is controlled by the Chamonix group, has been playing favorites all along. It was a big struggle just to get them to accept Edouin."

"But if they've already chosen someone, why don't they put his name in the papers?"

"Who knows? These things are never simple. We think that a group of famous men gets together and happily draws up a list; but it's never that easy. No, politics — that's what it's all about."

Whether it was really politics, or whether something

else was actually involved, no one could say. By the middle of February, only three weeks before the day of departure, the one remaining climber still had not been named to the team.

"Maybe they want a smaller group," Tricoussan said wisely. "Fewer climbers means less expense, and they're always trying to save a few francs. But if you have fewer people on the mountain, everyone has to work harder. Everyone has to take greater risks."

"I just hope it all works out," Louise commented; "I wish them luck, whoever they are."

Four days before the date of departure, there came an astonishing announcement. Not one, but two new climbers had been named to the expedition. Louise first heard about this at the Guides' Association office, where she had gone to meet a friend. As soon as she walked into the office, everyone shouted happily and broke into applause.

"But — what is this? What's this about?"

"Don't you know, Louise? Look," and someone handed her a newspaper.

In this way, she learned that a young guide from Montier, the daughter of a famous French mountaineer, had been selected as a new member of the national expedition. Departure had been put off for about another week — now they would sail on March 14, from Marseille.

"But that's impossible!" Louise exclaimed. "No — it simply can't be. It can't be!"

"But it *can* be, Louise! It's right there in black and white. How can you deny it?" said one of the guides.

"There must be a mistake. I don't understand how, after all that trouble, they could've chosen . . ."

In all the noise and excitement, with everyone shaking her hand and patting her on the back, she forgot to read the rest of the article. Later, when she had returned home, she read the name of the second climber who had been added to the expedition.

"Oh, no," she said with a groan. "Of all the people in the world! Why, it's Bruzel! Edouard Bruzel! I have to go talk to Father. I have to ask him what this means. Surely there's been a mistake, a big mistake. . . ."

Twenty

Unfortunately for Louise, there hadn't been a mistake. The other new member of the team was indeed Edouard Bruzel, the old guide who had given her so much trouble in the past. Now in his late fifties, Bruzel had retired from active guiding, but he remained an influential figure in French climbing circles. Just two years before, he had been named an associate director of the Alpine Club. Jules DeMaistre, who thought so little of Bruzel that he had once punched him in the nose, explained things this way:

"Louise, I had no choice — it was Bruzel, or no one else could've gone. I wanted you as part of the team from the start. But I knew they'd oppose me, so I pretended I didn't care. Then, when I finally had an opportunity, I arranged for my one friend in the Alpine Club, old Etienne Couzy, to put your name in nomination. But Bruzel saw the game I was playing, and he demanded that he, too, be included. He won't be climbing for the summit — his job is just to help me with supply problems."

"Well, I don't mind so much," Louise said doubtfully. "As long as I don't have to be on the same rope with him. I don't trust him."

"Neither do I. But if we play our cards right, he won't interfere. I'll keep him busy in the supply tent."

On March 14, the French team set sail. Twelve days later they landed in Bombay, India, from where they flew to Calcutta, one thousand miles to the east. In Calcutta all the equipment had to be sorted, repacked, and sent on to Kathmandu, in Nepal; in addition, a great quantity of food, more than three tons, had to be bought and packed in protective containers. Many nonperishable items had already been shipped from France, but here in Calcutta it was discovered that much had been stolen or damaged en route. Jules DeMaistre, who had a limited budget for making additional purchases, spent five days buying all the dehydrated food he could get his hands on. Bruzel, acting as assistant, proved surprisingly useful and resourceful in this effort.

"I'm encouraged, Louise," DeMaistre said to his daughter. "He never argues when I give an order, and he has real talent for organization. If anything should happen to me, I think he could take over very effectively."

"Nothing's going to happen to you. But you're already working harder than any of the others: why don't you send someone else down to the markets — me, for example, or Edouin?"

"No, I want you to stay with the other climbers. There's

a danger that they'll try to isolate you and Edouin — you, because you're a woman, and Edouin because he comes from Montier. I've asked all the climbers to work on one task, repacking the equipment. Stick to this, and don't worry about how hard I'm working."

In addition to eight official climbers (those who would go for the summit), the team included a doctor, a cameraman, and an interpreter. The doctor, Jean-Baptiste Truvette, was an expert in high-altitude medical problems (frostbite, cerebral and pulmonary edema, etc.). The cameraman, who had hoped to make a film for French television, unfortunately contracted amoebic dysentery and spent most of the trip in a hospital in Calcutta. The interpreter, a man named Louis Bontron, was fluent in nine languages, among them Hindustani and Nepali. His job was to make contact with the local officials, arrange for transportation, and hire porters and guides as they were needed.

Louise was the only woman among all these men. She was also the youngest member of the group, and she had to put up with a certain amount of teasing. But the biggest problem, as her father had anticipated, came from the Chamonix climbers: they tended to look down on anyone not from their own valley, which is the most famous climbing area in all Europe. For many years, there had been a rivalry between the guides of Chamonix and those of Montier. Jules DeMaistre, who had worked in Chamonix, was considered a "good fellow," even though he now belonged to the Montier Guides' Association; but Louise and Luc Edouin, who had grown up in Montier, were looked upon as distinct inferiors. Louise wasn't surprised by this type of behavior, and she treated it as a bad joke; but Luc was offended, and he got into some serious arguments with his Chamonix teammates (who, for their part, nicknamed him "The Green Stork," because of his long legs and extra-pale complexion).

"Louise, it's plain what they plan to do," Edouin said one night. "When we get on the mountain they'll make us carry all the heavy loads. But they won't let us push for the summit — only someone from Chamonix will be allowed to get to the top, you just watch."

"I don't know, Luc. Maybe you're right. But the mountains have a way of messing up such plans. What if only you or I were healthy enough to go for the top? That happens sometimes. When my father climbed on Kana Malu, in 1939, six of the seven members of his team got sick. He was the only one able to climb on the last day."

"Yes, Louise, but that was different. Your father hadn't exhausted himself early on, carrying heavy loads."

"Luc, we're not even in Nepal yet! And I haven't seen you carry anything heavier than a sleeping bag. My advice is: don't worry until you absolutely have to. Expect the best. Things generally work out."

From Calcutta, the team flew to Kathmandu, the capital of Nepal. Here they rented six trucks, which they loaded up with the food and equipment. The road leading out of Kathmandu was very rough, with gullies and large, sharp-edged boulders blocking the way. Two of the trucks broke down almost immediately, and it took the team four days to reach Pokhara, only eighty miles to the west. In the town of Pokhara, Louis Bontron hired two hundred Nepali porters to help carry the team's equipment. From here on, it would be impossible to move by car or truck: the "road" leading into the mountains was only a narrow path, very steep and rocky, with wild rivers to be crossed every few miles.

So far, the expedition had gone roughly according to schedule. (A few days had been lost getting to Pokhara, and a few more in Calcutta, but these delays had almost been expected.) It was very important that the team arrive at the base of Dhaulagiri by April 15. The actual climb, from the base to the top of the mountain, would take six weeks, and after that, the monsoon season, a time of severe and unrelenting storms, was due to start. Anyone caught on the mountain during that time would be in serious trouble. Just two years before, seven French climbers had frozen to death while coming down from the top of Dhaulagiri. Though well equipped with food, tents, and heavy clothing, they were pinned down by a blizzard that lasted seventeen days. (No one can survive for seventeen days at high altitude, no matter how well equipped.)

Jules DeMaistre knew all about the monsoon. But he was confident that they could reach the mountain early enough, and climb it quickly enough, to get away safely. However, a series of misfortunes now befell the French expedition. Three days out of Pokhara, one of the porters slipped while crossing a bamboo bridge over a river; swept away on the powerful current, he disappeared around a bend, and it took the team a full day to recover his body.

Then on the fifth day out, Edouard Bruzel and the Chamonix climbers left camp just before dinnertime. There was a little village nearby, and they had decided to eat supper there by themselves. Early the next morning, Bruzel and the others came down with terrible stomach cramps — apparently, something had been wrong with the food they ate in the village — and for the next two days they could only lie in their tents, groaning and clutching their bellies.

"Bruzel, I'm sorry to see you so under the weather," said Jules DeMaistre. "But remember that I warned you about eating the local food. People often get sick that way. Now we've lost another two days, and I'm starting to get worried."

"I'm so sorry, Jules — it was a stupid mistake. Believe me, I'm paying for it now. But why don't you and the others go on ahead? We'll catch up with you when we feel better. That is — if we ever do feel better. . . ."

With one thing and another, it wasn't until April 19 that the expedition finally arrived at Dhaulagiri. The severe, formidable peak rose before them now, its summit hidden in streaming clouds. The base of the mountain grew up from a jumbled wasteland of giant blocks of ice. Bruzel and the Chamonix climbers were almost completely recovered from their illness, but here, at eighteen thousand feet, everyone began to suffer from the extreme cold. That night, when Louise went to bed in her little tent, she couldn't stop shivering despite her excellent sleeping bag and several layers of extra clothing. If it was this cold at eighteen thousand feet, she wondered, what would it be like near the top, two miles higher up in the air?

Twenty-One

"Father — wake up! There's someone here to see you! He says it's important, very important!"

Louise, who had lain awake all night, had been up when a stranger stumbled into camp at around 4:00 A.M. The stranger, a Sherpa tribesman named Anshak Rana, had come down from Mount Changamal, some thirty miles to the northwest.

"He says there's been a terrible accident," Louise cried, shaking her father's tent. "The North Americans on Changamal — something bad's happened to them. Some sort of accident. They told him to run for help."

"All right, Louise — don't shake down my tent! I'll be out in a minute."

The Sherpa, who spoke almost no French, tried to explain to Louise what had happened on Changamal. From his wild gestures she gathered that there had been an avalanche, that several people had been buried, and that some others were badly injured. Fifteen minutes later, after hearing a translation of the man's story, Jules DeMaistre gathered all the members of his expedition together. He spoke calmly, but with an air of sadness.

"Yes, there's been an accident, a bad one. Five people lost in an avalanche. Another four with injuries, one of them with a broken back. One of the people killed was their medical officer, so Dr. Truvette will have to go back with the Sherpa. It's two days from here to Changamal, then another two days climbing on fixed ropes. The accident happened just above Camp Three, on the northwest face. It's a very dangerous area."

Dr. Truvette, who still looked sleepy (he had just come out of his tent), nodded automatically.

"I'll go back with Truvette," DeMaistre continued. "I'll take three of our own Sherpas, but I'll need three of our climbers, as well. If we can get the injured people off the mountain, we'll arrange for porters to carry them back to Pokhara. They can be evacuated out to Kathmandu from there."

Louise, listening carefully, looked puzzled as her father continued to speak. Two days getting to Changamal, then another two days getting to the accident site, plus more time spent evacuating the injured . . . this meant that their own climb, the ascent of Dhaulagiri, would have to be abandoned. There was no way to reach the injured climbers, then return to complete their climb before the monsoon arrived.

Even so, Louise raised her hand to volunteer. She said simply, "I'll go too. When do we start?"

"As soon as possible. And now — will anyone else come with us?" her father asked. "We need two more, I think."

"All right, all right. I'll go," volunteered Luc Edouin reluctantly, looking rather disappointed.

"Very good, Luc. And what about you, Maronnette? Will you join our little rescue party?"

Jean-François Maronnette, the youngest climber from Chamonix, lowered his eyes quickly.

"I don't know," he said after a moment. "I'm all for helping the Americans, of course, but what about us? What about our own plan? I came here for a particular reason: to climb Dhaulagiri, to climb to the top. It's very sad about the North Americans, but when you come to the mountains, you have to accept certain risks. Maybe the injured people are already dead. In that case, our rescue party will achieve nothing — just ruin our own chances of climbing."

Some of the other men, also from Chamonix, nodded sharply as Maronnette spoke. DeMaistre seemed very upset and angry for a moment; but then he also nodded.

"That's very true. All that you say is true, Maronnette. But if the situation were reversed, if we were the ones stuck up on Changamal, we'd be praying for the Americans to come help us. Wouldn't we? So speaking for myself, I know that I have to go. If no one else wants to come, that's all right, too. I understand."

For a long moment, there was complete silence in the

group. Jean-François Maronnette seemed to be struggling with himself — half of him wanted to volunteer, while the other half definitely did not. And now Edouard Bruzel, with a look of deep concern (as if it hurt him just to think about the poor, injured Americans), raised his hand.

"Of course, I'd like to volunteer. I feel a responsibility, a deep kinship, to our North American brothers. And let's not forget: most of us here are professional mountain guides. We've sworn to come to the aid of anyone in danger, no matter what the circumstances. Even though we've worked for a long time to get to this mountain, we have to think of the safety of those others. Yes — safety must always come first."

Jules DeMaistre seemed puzzled for a moment. Then he answered, "No, Bruzel — I can't let you come. Someone has to stay here and look after the supplies. While I'm gone, you'll be in charge of the expedition. I'm appointing you associate leader as of this moment."

As if surprised and disappointed, Bruzel shook his head and frowned. "I'd much rather be coming with you, Jules, you know that. But . . . I'll do as you say. All right: I'll look after the expedition, you can count on me."

"Very good. Then that's settled."

The group of climbers now dispersed.

Just before the rescue party left, DeMaistre took Bruzel aside and gave him some instructions.

"Start carrying loads up the mountain today, Edouard. Put Camp One at about nineteen thousand feet, Camp Two at twenty thousand, and so forth. In the time we're gone, you can fix ropes to all the lower slopes. Then when we get back, we'll join you at Camp Three or Four. We'll make the push for the summit together."

"Very good, Jules. I'll do exactly as you say."

"Yes, I know you will. But listen closely now, Edouard. I know what's going on in the back of your mind. You think that as soon as we leave, you can take over, and you and your Chamonix climbers can reach the summit without us. That may very well be what happens in the end. But I'm warning you: as associate leader, you're responsible for the lives of these men. Since I'm taking Truvette along with me, you won't have a medical officer in your group. That means that if anything goes wrong, you'll have to deal with the consequences yourself."

"Yes, yes," said Bruzel nervously. "But I wasn't thinking of . . . why, I would never dream of taking your place, never. . . ."

"Never mind — I don't really care, Bruzel. It's all the same to me. If we don't come back in a week, do as you wish. Go for the summit if you want. But remember — this mountain is treacherous. Things can go wrong so easily up there. There's the weather, and then there's the mountain itself — it's a different world above twenty thousand feet. So cold, so harsh . . . may God protect you."

Twenty-Two

At the last moment, someone else joined the little rescue party. It was Jean-François Maronnette, who had decided to come along to Changamal after all. "I just wouldn't feel right," he said, "thinking about you up there. Worrying about the rescue. And if we get back soon enough, we'll still have a chance to climb Dhaulagiri."

"Don't count on it," answered Edouin gloomily. "There's no way to get back in a week — simply no way. We've lost our chance at Dhaulagiri, that's for sure."

"Oh, Luc, how do you know?" asked Louise. "You're such a pessimist. At least we're here in the Himalayas, where we've always wanted to come. Can't you enjoy that, at least?"

"I'm trying," Edouin answered flatly. "Believe me, Louise — I'm trying."

Despite her own optimism, Louise soon began to feel that Edouin was probably right. The walk from Dhaulagiri into the Changamal massif took three days, not two, and conditions were very rough. Each morning brought sharp, cold weather, with piercingly clear skies overhead; then at around two o'clock each afternoon, a storm blew in, and the party had to stop to make camp quickly, usually in an uncomfortable position on a ridge. The next morning, there would be a foot or two of fresh snow on the ground, which made walking more difficult. This weather pattern of cold, clear mornings, followed by storms in the afternoon, was normal for that part of the Himalaya, but Jules DeMaistre was worried anyway.

"I don't like how cold it is," he said. "And how strong the storms are, even at the lower elevations. It could mean that the monsoon's arriving early this year."

"What about the people up on Changamal?" wondered Louise. "It must be even worse where they are."

"Yes, much worse. I'm afraid for them, Louise — I don't see how they can survive."

On the morning of the fourth day, Louise stepped out of her tent just before dawn. Yawning and shivering at the same time, she suddenly caught sight of Changamal, the Blue Lioness, in the near distance, and she made a funny sound, a cry of fear and delight mixed together. The graceful, mysterious-looking mountain, as it rose up in the cold, early-morning light, looked like an enormous jewel seen through clear water. Every feature of its northwest face was sharply defined, and the beautiful detail of its ridges, glaciers, and blue-tinted ice walls filled her with a sort of terrified happiness.

"Yes, I can see why they call you the Lioness," she said softly, as if the mountain were listening to her. "You're so beautiful, and . . . so female. Yes — definitely female. You look like the queen of all the mountains in the world. I can't believe that people actually dare to climb you."

"Never by the northwest face," commented Maronnette, who had just gotten out of his own tent. "That's where those poor North Americans are stranded. Look, Louise — do you see the avalanche cone? That whole side of the mountain looks like a death trap."

Later that morning, the party reached the base camp of the North American expedition. Nothing had been heard from the stranded climbers for several days; the porters were afraid to climb up to them, and the Sherpas who had taken supplies up two days before hadn't returned. The rescue party set out immediately, climbing along the ropes that had been fixed on the mountain. Luckily, the storm arrived a little late that afternoon, at three o'clock; DeMaistre's group had just reached Camp 2 when the clouds blew in, and snow was soon falling thickly.

Louise had never been at this great an altitude before. She had a constant headache (a common symptom of altitude sickness), she felt weak all over, and she had to force herself to eat when dinner was ready. When she lay down in her tent, she had the feeling that something kept her from breathing; an invisible hand seemed to be pressing on her chest, preventing her from ever getting a full, satisfying breath. All around her tent the storm howled and screamed, and she heard avalanches all through the night. The path of the avalanches lay seventy yards to the right of the camp, so there was no danger of being buried; but the force of the avalanches was frightening, like an earthquake that kept shaking the mountain from within.

In the morning, Louise could hardly get out of her sleeping bag, she felt so weak. Every muscle in her body was sore, and the simple effort of sitting up left her breathless. When Anshak Rana, the Sherpa guide, brought her a cup of tea, he immediately recognized her condition, and he went to fetch Dr. Truvette, who advised her not to climb that day.

"It's just the altitude," he explained. "Your body isn't used to it yet. The air contains so little oxygen that your lungs have to strain to work. Edouin also doesn't feel well, and even your father looks tired. I've told him that the whole team should spend the day in the tents, resting."

"But what about the North Americans? We can't waste a day resting. They might die at any moment."

"That's true. And of course your father rejected my advice. He's getting ready to leave right now. I'll go along with him, and Maronnette will probably come too. But you and Edouin shouldn't move. You can follow us tomorrow if you're better."

Though disappointed, Louise knew that she was in no shape to climb that day. If she had tried, she would have caused many problems for the other team members. So she stayed in her tent all morning, forcing herself to eat and to drink many cups of tea. (At high altitudes, the air is so dry that it draws all the moisture out of the human body, and death from dehydration is not uncommon.) At 3:30 that afternoon, Jean-François Maronnette came down from the area above Camp 3. The rescue party had found the injured climbers: all of them were alive, although the man with a broken back was in bad shape. He would have to be carried down the mountain on a stretcher. The other three had broken arms, shoulder and knee sprains, and possible internal injuries. One of the climbers had been unconscious for several days: he had just come out of his coma when the rescue team arrived.

"This is amusing, Louise," Maronnette said. "You'll like this. As soon as the guy sees your father, he rushes up and hugs him, and then he begins putting a pack of equipment together. Your father asks him where he thinks he's going, and he says, 'Why, up the mountain. We still have to establish Camp Four and, after that, Camp Five. Then we can go for the summit.' Your father explained that there had been an avalanche, that five of his teammates had been killed. Didn't he remember? Then the poor guy gets a horrified look on his face, and he breaks down completely. You see — he'd forgotten all about it. It just slipped his mind."

"Well, I'm not sure I find that so funny," Louise answered. "Is this man all right? Has he got a serious head injury?"

"No, Dr. Truvette checked him out. He's okay. I tell you, Louise, these North Americans don't impress me much, not at all. I've had worse injuries myself and still been able to climb. But they just sat there, waiting to die. Thank God we came along."

The next morning, feeling much better herself, Louise began the climb to Camp 3. Halfway there she met Anshak Rana, who was breaking trail through the snow for the rescuers bringing down the man with the broken back. Then a few minutes later, continuing on up, she met two of the Sherpas and Dr. Truvette. The man with the broken back was strapped to a stretcher; Truvette and the others were lowering him carefully along the ropes, and it seemed that they would be able to get him down to Camp 2. Louise offered to help, but Truvette told her to continue on to the higher camp, where her father was.

Here she found two of the North Americans getting ready to descend. One had an aluminum splint on his leg, the other a splint on both an arm and a leg. Jules DeMaistre, coming out of one of the tents at that moment, beckoned to his daughter. He asked her how she was feeling.

"Much better, thanks. Even my headache's gone. Can I help you? I heard about the man with the head injury. Is he really all right?"

"He's just a little dehydrated, that's all. But I wanted to talk to you about that, Louise. You see — there's something funny about this guy. Prepare yourself for a shock."

"A shock?"

"Yes. He's over there, in the small blue tent. He asked to see you."

"To see me? Why?"

Since DeMaistre would say no more, Louise went over to the tent. She tapped on the door flap. When no one answered, she looked inside. A man was lying on a sleeping mat, his body turned away from her. Now he rolled slowly in her direction. As he did so, his eyes opened halfway — he seemed very tired, very weak.

Then Louise recognized him — it was Lawrence Darnley — and she gasped. Her hand flew up to her throat, and she drew back. Lawrence just stared at her, not speaking, not even blinking. But he finally reached out and took her hand. This effort seemed all that he could manage; he closed his eyes again, murmured something she couldn't understand, and fell asleep.

Twenty-Three

The North American expedition to Changamal had been jinxed from the start. The weather had been very bad; hundreds of pounds of supplies had been lost or stolen; and the team members, from the United States and Canada, had argued among themselves from the first day. The team leader (one of the five killed in the avalanche) had never directed an expedition before this one, and his lack of experience had harmed the group effort. Then, just when things were starting to work, when the real climbing was about to begin, the avalanche came.

"And the deaths could've been avoided — they were completely unnecessary," said Lawrence bitterly, two days after his rescue. "It was obvious that the slope above Camp Three was dangerous — anyone could see there was going to be a great avalanche there. I warned Sibley, our leader, that we had to go over to the west, where the climbing was harder but safer. Not only didn't he listen — he sent people across the snowfield only a few yards apart. That way, when the avalanche came, it wiped out everyone all at once. The whole group of us."

Lawrence was very angry about the accident. (Down at base camp, he had quickly recovered his strength; the three other men had been evacuated out to Pokhara.) Though he had warned the others about the avalanche, he blamed himself for what happened; after all, the idea for climbing the northwest face had originally been his. Louise was afraid, at first, that he was going a little crazy — he talked about the accident constantly, and he refused to be taken out to Pokhara. He wanted to stay there on Changamal, in sight of the Blue Lioness, even though the French rescuers were getting ready to return to Dhaulagiri.

"After so many lives have been lost, I can't just give it up," he explained. "Then the others will have died for nothing. And we almost made it — we established camps all the way up to twenty-three thousand feet. All we'd have to do is to restock the camps. Anshak Rana says he'll stay with me, and I can probably get a couple of other Sherpas. We have plenty of equipment and food. With some luck, we could be on the summit in four days."

Louise merely shook her head. This idea seemed preposterous to her. But she knew how determined Lawrence could be; after all, he was the man who first climbed the Devil's Slide (with a little help from her, of course). On the day when Louise and the others were about to leave, Lawrence surprised her by saying:

"I know how you feel about me, Louise — I know you don't like me, that you find my company distasteful. But you're my only hope. I think we could make it to the top — you, me, Anshak Rana, and one other man. I need one experienced climber with me. I can't do it just with the Sherpas."

"But Lawrence — I don't know what you mean. Why do you say I don't like you, that I find your company distasteful?"

"Never mind about that. That's all in the past. I'm asking you just as a comrade — as a fellow mountaineer. Please, help us get to the top. For the sake of all the people who died, if for no other reason."

"But Lawrence, I've never disliked you, not at all. And . . . but this is impossible. We could never make the top. You know it would take a minimum of ten of us, plus Sherpas, to climb a mountain like Changamal. Think of all the loads we'd have to carry."

"Yes, we'd have to carry extra loads. But with fewer people we could go more quickly. And if we only stayed up a few days, we wouldn't need so much food. We'd only have to carry one or two double loads. I think we could do it. Yes — I'm sure of it."

In his enthusiasm, Lawrence didn't wait to hear what else Louise had to say. He rushed off to find Jules DeMaistre, to explain his daring plan. DeMaistre listened closely, nodding thoughtfully; he smoked his pipe for a minute or two, then he said:

"It's a good plan, yes. An intriguing idea. The only

problem is the weather. If you get caught near the summit by a storm, without extra food or someone to come rescue you, well. . . ."

"Yes, I've thought of that. I've already planned for that. We'll carry extra food and bivouac gear, even on the summit push. We won't be caught out unprepared, I promise."

"With no one to come to your rescue," DeMaistre persisted, "and no way to get a message off the mountain, it would be bad if you had any sort of accident. But I think you really might make it. The fixed ropes are still on the mountain. And we've left all the tents and some gear at Camps Two and Three. The Sherpas are strong climbers, you can trust them. But I think you should take someone else along. Maybe Luc Edouin."

"Oh, I've already asked someone else. You see — I've already asked Louise."

At that moment, Louise approached the two men. Jules DeMaistre looked at her in alarm; then he looked back at Lawrence. His mouth fell open, and his face turned slightly pale.

"Will you do it, Louise?" Lawrence inquired. "Will you go with me — will you climb the mountain?"

"I don't know, Lawrence. It still seems risky. I don't want to be hasty about such a decision. And . . . I'm still a member of the Dhaulagiri team. My father would have to give his permission for me to come."

"Oh — your father just said that it's a good plan. He said I could ask Edouin to come, but since you and I have climbed together, I think we'd make a much stronger team.

Well, is it settled, then? Can we start packing the equipment, get ready to leave?"

Still slightly pale, Jules DeMaistre forced himself to nod assent. The idea of sending his daughter on such an adventure filled him with fear — the dangers were too many, the chances for disaster too great. But Louise was a grown woman now; she knew her own mind. If this was what she wanted, he couldn't stand in her way. And yet, the whole time she was gone, he was sure to be worried, sick with worry. . . .

Twenty-Four

On the afternoon of May 4, 1960, the Darnley expedition reoccupied Camp 3 on Changamal. The last few days had been spent hauling loads up the fixed ropes; Louise had carried a heavy pack each day, but she was stronger now, she was getting used to the altitude. The team consisted of six people at this point. In addition to Darnley, Louise, and three Sherpas, Jean-François Maronnette had decided to join up, and his presence was to prove very important. The work of stocking five camps, each one higher than the next, was a great burden, and Maronnette was a dependable climber who never complained. Without his help, the team would never have come close to reaching the summit.

On the afternoon of May 4, no storm blew in. This was the first time in weeks that the weather had stayed clear all day. Darnley guessed that it would be good for some days, and he pushed the team to seize the opportunity. On the fifth, they climbed fifteen hundred vertical feet, finally reaching a ledge where they established Camp 4. In the early morning, the thermometer read minus twenty-four degrees Fahrenheit, and Louise found that her climbing boots, which she normally put inside her sleeping bag to keep warm, had frozen solid as wood. It took her an hour to thaw them and get them on. But later that same morning, two hundred yards above Camp 4, she thought that she would die from the heat. The sun at that altitude, as it reflected off the snow, was so intense that her body was drenched in sweat. Climbing on a rope with Maronnette, she led a hard pitch up a wall of blue ice. Maronnette put several pitons in the wall, to belay her if she fell; but they both knew that any mistake at that altitude would probably mean death.

"Beautiful lead," Maronnette said, after Louise had finished and he had followed her. "You climb as well as anyone I've ever seen, man or woman, boy or girl. How do you feel? Are you tired?"

"A little. But I'm cold, that's the main thing. As soon as you get out of the sun, the sweat freezes against your skin. It's like wearing an undershirt made of ice."

"We'd better keep moving. I'll lead for a while. Just a bit farther . . ."

After reaching a sort of ridge, they climbed back down to Camp 4. The next day, the rest of the team would climb the route that they had established, using the steps they had cut and the ropes that they'd attached to the wall.

Though she had been in the mountains all her life,

Louise was unprepared for the size and scale of the Himalayas. When the weather was clear, she could see hundreds of miles to the north, west, and east, far into Nepal and Tibet. The feeling of being at the top of the world was overwhelming, and sometimes she shuddered with a kind of frightened happiness. It was the same mix of emotions she had felt when she saw Changamal at dawn. The world of the high peaks was supremely beautiful — everything was perfectly clean, sharply outlined, immense.

One day, carrying a load up to Camp 4, she set out at about eight o'clock, expecting to arrive before noon. In the snowfield above her was a small black rock: she could see each detail, each crack and bump on its surface. Telling herself that the rock was only about a hundred yards away, she began to walk uphill. After an hour of steady progress, she looked for the rock again — and it was still about a hundred yards away, still about the same size! Yet when she looked behind her, she saw that she had come a good distance up from Camp 3. She put her head down and began walking again through the soft snow. After another hour and a half, she looked for the rock — now it was at least a little closer (although still a good distance off).

Four hours after setting out, just after noon, she finally arrived at the black rock. But it wasn't small — on the contrary, it was enormous, one of the tallest, most massive boulders she had ever seen. Only the clarity of the atmosphere, and the tremendous scale of Changamal itself, had made the rock seem small and fairly close. After this experience, Louise was careful to estimate distances more generously. Something that seemed close at hand, only a stone's throw uphill, almost always turned out to be miles and miles away.

"Louise, you climb well with Maronnette," Lawrence said one evening. (It was the night of May 11. They had finally established Camp 5, the last one before the summit.)

"He's very good," she answered. "Very strong; and the altitude doesn't seem to bother him."

"That's why I've decided . . . well, you see, I think you and Maronnette should go for the summit together. I'll climb behind, with Anshak Rana. If you make it up safely, and if the weather holds, we'll also give it a try. It would be great if all four of us could get to the top."

"Yes — it would be great, all right."

But later that night, as they were lying in their sleeping bags, listening to the thundering of avalanches, Louise said:

"I don't know — I'm not sure I should go for the top. *You* should climb with Maronnette, Lawrence . . . after all, it's your expedition. You know more about the headwall than anybody. What if Maronnette and I go up and can't find the route — what if we get stuck just below the summit?"

"You won't get stuck, Louise. You've been finding routes all over the mountain, even where I couldn't see them. I have complete confidence in you — and it would give me great pleasure, really great pleasure, to see you on top. I'd almost rather have you get there than get there myself."

The next morning, Maronnette and Anshak Rana climbed up from Camp 4. There had been a heavy snowfall during the night, and when the two men arrived, they were exhausted from wading through snow above their waists. Maronnette immediately went to lie down in one of the tents. When Lawrence went to talk to him later, he found Maronnette groaning and holding his stomach.

"It started last night . . . throwing up, diarrhea, fever. That walk through the snow nearly killed me."

"All right, I'll get you some pills. Hold on."

After treating Maronnette with antibiotics and fluids, Lawrence told Louise that they would have to wait now. Camp 5 was located at 26,700 feet. At that altitude, any sickness can quickly become life threatening, and if Maronnette did not improve, they would have to take him down the mountain, to a lower altitude, where the higher oxygen content of the air would aid recovery.

By the middle of the afternoon, however, Maronnette was in less pain. By early evening, when it had begun to snow again, his fever had subsided, and he seemed to be resting comfortably. Lawrence decided that it wouldn't be necessary to carry him down the mountain after all. As long as he continued improving, he could stay at Camp 5, and he still might be able to go for the summit later.

"But Lawrence — we can't wait for him to get better. The weather's changing already," Louise warned. "Today's storm came in earlier than yesterday's, and tomorrow's will be earlier still."

"Well, that's right. But so what? What can I do about the weather?"

"You can't do anything about the weather, but you can change the climbing teams, Lawrence. Send someone else to the top, in place of Maronnette. It's essential."

"No — that wouldn't be right. You and Maronnette are our two strongest climbers, and I have a responsibility to send the two best. We have to wait for him to get better, that's all."

"But I'm not going to wait, Lawrence — I'm not. If the weather's clear tomorrow, I'm going for the summit, by myself if necessary. I haven't come thousands of miles just to get snowed in fifteen hundred feet below the top."

"Louise — I can't let you go alone. You know that. It just wouldn't be safe."

"In that case — protect me. Help me, Lawrence . . . give me someone else to climb with. Someone I know well. Someone I've climbed with before . . . someone I trust and like. . . ."

Twenty-Five

Thus it was that on May 13, 1960, at 3:30 in the morning, Louise set out with Lawrence Darnley as her climbing partner. Their objective: the summit of Changamal (28,114 feet).

They carried very little gear. Lawrence had a small camera, for taking pictures if they got to the top; he also brought along food, a rope, ice and rock pitons, and extra clothing. Louise carried supplies for making a bivouac, in case they failed to return to camp before dark. Each was wearing bulky, insulated snow clothing. They had hoods over their heads, dark glasses to protect their eyes, heavy mittens on their hands, and oversized boots that came up to their knees. They wore crampons on their boots and each carried an ice ax.

To climb fifteen hundred feet — about a quarter of a

mile — hardly seems much of a challenge. But at the top of the world, any movement is terribly hard. Louise took a deep breath with every step; each one felt like the toughest thing she had ever done in her life. Soon she was taking two breaths per step, and she rested every three or four minutes. The cold was deadly; if, by some accident, one of her mittens had fallen off, her hand would have frozen solid in less than a minute, just like her boots on that morning when she forgot to put them in her sleeping bag. The cold penetrated her snowsuit, her underclothes, her mittens, and her boots; the only thing making it bearable was the physical activity of climbing, which heated her from within.

Just above Camp 5, a snowfield stretched away to the foot of a glacier. In the dark of early morning, Lawrence led them around the side of the glacier; then, as the sky started to lighten, he climbed onto the ice field's surface, with Louise following on the rope. From the glacier they could see the headwall of Changamal. It was a bleak, ice-covered rock face, overhanging and severe.

"No — it can't be," Louise said to herself. "It's not possible to climb that — not at this altitude."

Lawrence must have had the same feeling. He kept staring at the wall, shaking his head and saying nothing. But after a minute, he started trudging forward again, determined to give the wall a try, at least. The glacier was full of crevasses, frightening splits in the ice, some of them hundreds of feet deep. Lawrence moved very carefully, testing the surface ahead of him before each step. Usually the crevasses were easy to see, but sometimes the snow had blown over the openings, and a careless step would have plunged both of them into the icy blue depths.

"Please," Louise found herself praying, "don't let me die here — not in one of these horrible ice caverns. If I have to die, let it be up on that wall, out in the clear, open air. With the sky and mountains all around."

Slowly, cautiously, they made their way over the glacier. Now they had to stop and rest every other minute; they would walk a short distance, then fall to their knees, gasping for air. Eventually they arrived at the base of the headwall. Lawrence began searching to his right and left; suddenly he signaled to Louise: he had found something. In the photographs he had studied of the face, he had noticed a dark line going up the middle of the headwall. This line was a series of cracks, which led to a steep couloir, a gully worn in the rock by avalanches and icefall. If they could climb up the cracks, they would arrive at the bottom of the couloir. From there, it led up to the summit ridge.

"But you have to lead the crack, Louise," Lawrence shouted over the wind. "I can't do it. You're our only chance."

"All right. All right, I'll give it a try."

Louise began inching up the first crack. It was full of smooth ice, and her crampons were all that saved her from falling. Unfortunately, the ice was too thin to take the bit of her ice ax; the ice shattered with each blow. But she had climbed in such conditions before, she told herself. In fact, she had been doing this all her life: moving up cautiously, maintaining her balance at all times, refusing to panic, no matter what. The crack disappeared at one point, and luckily she found a way to use her ice ax at just that place. Strangely enough, she began to feel better than she had down on the glacier; she was still gasping for air, but for a good reason now, because she was climbing as hard as she could, using all her strength and powers of concentration. At the end of the first pitch, she brought Lawrence up to her belay position. He climbed slowly but well, and when he arrived beside her he had a big, crazy smile on his face.

"Louise, I can't believe it! I think we might actually do this! I think we're going to make it!"

"Not so fast — we still have two pitches more. But if you're feeling so positive, Lawrence, why don't you lead this next part? Up that diagonal crack?"

"Yes — absolutely!"

Standing below him, watching him struggle up the narrow crack, Louise began to be infected by his enthusiasm. Just for a moment, she felt the way she had years ago, when they climbed the Devil's Slide together. On that climb, she had been happier than ever before in her life; she had been doing what she most loved to do, and doing it with him, with this one man she felt something special about. For those few hours, she had believed that her whole life made a kind of sense, that it was starting to come true, like a story she had read in a book of magical tales. But when that climb was over, when Lawrence suddenly turned from her, acting as if they had only been teammates, climbing partners and nothing more — that disappointment had hurt her deeply, more deeply than she knew at the time. She had turned away from the very idea of happiness after that, seeing it as something dangerous. Never again would she let herself be so open — so available to disappointment. If she had to live without happiness . . . well, at least she would live.

But the feeling she had now — a return of all the old, openhearted enthusiasm — was strong. The beautiful day on the mountain was like the weather inside of her, and she no longer felt the need to protect herself, to guard against disappointment. When Lawrence completed his long pitch, Louise climbed up next to him, and then she continued up the couloir. Stinging showers of snow kept blowing down the gully. She had to climb into these mini-avalanches, kicking with her crampons and using her ax in the thick, blue-tinted ice. When she reached the top of the couloir, she was covered with ice and snow, white from head to foot. Half blinded by the snow, she kicked her way up the left side of the gully, and after pulling around an overhanging block of ice, she crawled onto the summit ridge.

Still half blinded, she quickly established a belay and brought Lawrence up on the rope. When he emerged from the couloir, the wind suddenly quieted. Just for a moment the summit itself came into view — they could see it directly ahead of them, looking near enough to touch.

Twenty-Six

While Louise and Lawrence were climbing on Changamal, moving steadily toward the summit, Jules DeMaistre returned to Dhaulagiri. The rescue effort had taken longer than expected, and DeMaistre wasn't surprised to find that the French team, under Bruzel's direction, had pushed on for the top of the mountain. But the weather on Dhaulagiri was very bad that year — it had taken Bruzel and the Chamonix climbers longer than expected to reach Camps 2 and 3, and only now, when DeMaistre had returned, were they ready to climb higher.

Upon his arrival at base camp, DeMaistre spoke to Bruzel over the shortwave radio (Bruzel was at Camp 3). The conversation went like this:

Bruzel: Glad you're back, Jules, very glad. Please supervise restocking of the lower camps. We'll be pushing on up tomorrow. . . .

DeMaistre: You only have a short time left before the monsoon, Edouard. How is everybody? Everybody in fairly good shape?

Bruzel: Yes, pretty good. Haussmann has the flu or something, and one of the Sherpas sprained his shoulder the other day, but that's all. Oh, if only this damned weather would break. We expect a bad storm again tonight. I don't see how the monsoon could be any worse than this — we couldn't climb yesterday or the day before. Lots of avalanches, too.

Indeed, that night, a storm blew in that lasted for five days straight. Bruzel and the other climbers were stuck at Camp 3, unable to move up or down. On the fifth day, DeMaistre and Luc Edouin managed to get to Camp 2, where they left fresh supplies. They spent the night at 2, then retreated to base camp in near-blizzard conditions. The storm wiped out all shortwave communication on the mountain. But finally, on the afternoon of May 17, DeMaistre was able to get through on the radio again:

DeMaistre: I think you'd better come down now, Bruzel . . . the summit's clearly out of the question. How are the men feeling?

Bruzel: Well, some are pretty weak. I'm sending Haussmann down with two of the others, plus two Sherpas. We're running out of food here . . . thank God you brought those supplies up to Camp 2. Some of these fellows have a lot of heart, despite their condition. They still want to climb higher. . . .

DeMaistre: Listen, Edouard — don't be foolish. You can't climb higher — you have to come down, and soon. I don't care how much heart the men have. This isn't a question of heart, or bravery, or anything like that — there's just no way to reach the summit. As the leader of this expedition, I'm ordering you to retreat. Start coming down as soon as possible. . . .

Bruzel: I'm sorry — could you repeat that, Jules? I didn't hear you. Something must be wrong with the radio . . . yes, please repeat. . . .

Jules DeMaistre was never to know if the radio actually went bad at that point, or if Bruzel was only pretending not to hear him. No matter how many times he tried to call over the next few days, he could never get an answer; and when Haussmann, the sick climber, arrived at base camp, DeMaistre had to give all his attention to caring for him. (Gérard Haussmann, age twenty-seven, was suffering from spinal meningitis, not the flu. After being evacuated out he spent six weeks in a hospital in Kathmandu, where he eventually recovered.) On the morning of May 21, the weather suddenly cleared, and DeMaistre, Luc Edouin, and Dr. Truvette began to organize another rescue party. On the afternoon of the twenty-third, they reached Camp 3, only to find it abandoned. It appeared that Bruzel and the four remaining climbers had pushed on for the summit — despite the weather, despite their weakened condition, and despite DeMaistre's warnings.

Three of the climbers were never found. (In all probability, they died above 25,500 feet, after establishing Camps 4 and 5.) But after an exhaustive search of the mountain, once again in windy, stormy conditions, DeMaistre located the bodies of Edouard Bruzel and René Devoussaud (age twenty-six). Both men had frozen to death. What was curious about their condition was this: Devoussaud, the smaller man, was cradled in the arms of the larger one, Bruzel. They had begun the descent from Camp 4 together, probably after witnessing the deaths of their three companions. But halfway down to Camp 3, and probable safety, Devoussaud collapsed, too weak to go any farther. Bruzel, rather than abandon his partner to certain death, picked him up and carried him several hundred yards in his arms. Then — finally exhausted himself — Bruzel also collapsed in the snow.

In all likelihood, if Bruzel had not tried to save his friend, he would have reached Camp 3, and he would have survived. This is why Jules DeMaistre, in the official report he later wrote about the expedition, described Bruzel as "a hero — yes, a true hero, despite the terrible outcome of our venture. Because a hero is not necessarily a man who achieves his goal, but rather one who forgets about himself; who sees the task before him and, with no concern for his own safety, pushes onward. Edouard Bruzel cared less, in those final moments, for his own survival than for that of his climbing companion. And by this unselfish act he proved himself to be a true mountaineer: one who goes far beyond the range of normal, mortal men. . . ."

Twenty-Seven

Louise and Lawrence, of course, knew nothing of the tragedy happening on Dhaulagiri. Their own harrowing experience, on Changamal, was taking place at about the same time.

The sky was a dark, fathomless blue — the snowy ridge pure white, whiter than whipped cream. Louise had lost all sense of physical effort; she knew that she was still moving, still trudging steadily upward, but she seemed to be standing outside herself, calmly watching.

Lawrence was about ten yards ahead of her. He was slowly, laboriously breaking a path through the deep snow. The ridge itself was only a few yards wide at this point — if Lawrence had moved to either side, he would have fallen off, tumbled into empty space.

Suddenly he stopped moving forward. Louise kept on

walking, but it took her a long time to catch up to him; climbing was easy now, but everything moved so slowly, took years and years to happen. Finally, as she was reaching out to touch Lawrence on the shoulder, to ask him why he had stopped, he turned around. He pulled her toward him, grabbed her in a clumsy embrace. Then she understood. There was absolutely nothing ahead of him, nowhere else to climb, no higher ground. They were standing on the summit itself.

"Louise . . . Louise!" was all he could say, his voice strangled by emotion. And after a while she answered:

"Yes, it's all right, Lawrence. We've done it, haven't we? Yes, we've really done it, I think."

But this was no place to linger. Lawrence took a few photographs; he seemed to have trouble operating his camera, and at one point, one of his mittens fell into the snow. He continued using his camera, and Louise hurriedly grabbed the mitten and forced him to put it back on. (In only seconds, his fingers would have begun to freeze, and the hand might have needed to be amputated later.) This problem with his mitten frightened Louise more than anything, more even than the fearful precipice on which they stood: it meant that they were becoming confused, that their minds were being affected by the extreme altitude.

"Lawrence — we have to head down now," she shouted. "Immediately — there's no time to waste."

"Yes, yes. In a minute, Louise. Look — you can see all around us. To the very ends of the earth."

They had brought along two flags, one Canadian, one

French. Louise planted these pennants in the frozen snow. Then she tied herself and Lawrence into the rope. It took forever to make the knots; her hands were clumsy, and she kept forgetting what she was doing, losing her train of thought. Lawrence tried to help her, but his efforts were worse than useless. Finally they were roped up, and Louise led the way, back down the snowy ridge.

The weather had begun to change. It was one o'clock in the afternoon, and storm clouds were already forming. Louise followed the path they had made coming up, but it was blown over in places, completely hidden by drifted snow. They reached the top of the headwall just after two o'clock. At first, she couldn't find the couloir they had climbed coming up; her plan was to rappel down the wall, exactly reversing the route they had used. But she became confused now — she felt more and more desperate. Then, just by luck, she stumbled on the opening of the couloir.

"Lawrence, shall I go down first?"

"I don't know. Whatever you want, Louise. . . ."

She was worried about him. He had a thoughtful, peaceful expression on his face, but when he tried to speak, he often didn't make sense. At every opportunity he lay down in the snow to rest. Now Louise had to decide on her own: Was Lawrence alert enough to handle himself, to rappel down the ropes on the steep headwall? And if he wasn't, what was she supposed to do then? She couldn't just carry him. And she doubted that she was strong enough to lower him all the way on the rope.

"Lawrence, listen to me. You have to listen . . . we're

going to die if we don't act quickly. We have to get back down the couloir. We'll go together — you first, then me right behind you. I'll tie us together in case you slip on the rope. You have to rappel down *now*, Lawrence . . . Lawrence, do you hear me?"

Once again, he had lain down in the snow. He curled up on his side, closing his eyes as if to go to sleep. Louise had to attach his rappel device to the rope herself. Then she attached her own device. Using a short length of material called a sling, she tied herself to Lawrence; in this way, if he lost hold of his device, or if he became unconscious, she would still be able to stop his slide along the rope.

"All right, Lawrence. You first."

"No . . . it's too beautiful. So beautiful up here. I don't ever want to go down. . . ."

"Get hold of yourself, Lawrence — come on! Take a step backward. There — that's right. You're on rappel now."

Halfway down the steep couloir, Lawrence let go of the rope. The full weight of his body immediately pulled against Louise, and she was only barely able to control their slide along the doubled ropes. Clouds and stinging showers of blown snow obscured the headwall. Louise prayed that she would be able to recognize the ledge where they had to stop first — they had to make the descent in several stages, since the ropes were only sixty yards long. So far, the anchor above them, to which the doubled ropes were attached, was holding. But the weight of two people on a single rappel line was excessive, it greatly increased their danger. Suddenly, she felt Lawrence stirring below her. He had started to wake up, to rappel on his own again; this was a great relief, since it meant that she no longer had to support his weight.

"All right, Lawrence — we're almost there. Look for the ledge at the top of the crack. I don't know if I can find it myself. . . ."

Though it was still midafternoon, night seemed to have fallen. The clouds that swirled around them were dark and dense, full of freezing moisture. It suddenly began to snow — a heavy, blanketing snow, snow so thick that the air itself was hard to breathe. They luckily found the little ledge, tied themselves on to it, and quickly established a second rappel. Louise could no longer feel either her fingers or her toes. She had always been especially afraid of frostbite; one of her father's oldest friends, a retired guide from a valley near Montier, had lost all his toes and several fingers to frostbite, and she remembered, as a little girl, being horrified the first time she saw one of his bare, mutilated feet. It had looked so unnatural, like a club made out of skin — more like an elephant's foot than something belonging to a human being. "Oh, well" (she said to herself, in the freezing storm), "there's nothing I can do about it now: either I'll lose my fingers and toes, or I won't. . . ."

In the darkness, in the fierce, freezing storm, the two climbers slid silently along the ropes. Below them they could make out nothing, only a murky, swirling chaos.

Twenty-Eight

"Lawrence, get up! We have to move!"

"Just a minute. Only a minute more, Louise. . . ."

They had made it — they had reached the bottom of the headwall. Camp 5 was less than six hundred yards away. If they could get there they would be safe; now, they only had to cross the glacier.

But Lawrence had sat down in the snow again. The problem was his feet, he explained: he had lost all feeling in them, and now, in the raging storm, he was trying to take off his boots, to pound and massage his feet, to bring back circulation.

"Lawrence — not now. Not here. We have to get to Camp Five as soon as possible."

"But I can't feel them, Louise. I can't walk this way. . . ."

Somehow, she forced him to get up. She convinced

him that though he might save his feet, the rest of him would die if they didn't keep moving. They plunged on into the storm. In the thick darkness, Louise tried to remember the route they had followed to get to the bottom of the headwall. They had crossed a snowfield, then they had walked along the glacier, before climbing up onto its surface. If they could follow the same path heading back, but in reverse, they would arrive safely at camp.

But the storm was getting much worse. They could hardly see, and powerful winds almost blew them off their feet. Lawrence was walking just behind her, attached to her by the rope. Sometimes he disappeared completely in the swirling ice and snow. Under the best of conditions, there was always a great danger crossing a glacier; under these conditions, it was almost a certainty that they would lose their way, stumble into a crevasse.

Nevertheless, Louise led on for as long as she could. She could see no alternative, and by thinking hard and picturing the route that they had followed that morning, she could usually remember the location of the largest crevasses. Now, though, the crevasses were hidden by snow; Louise used her ice ax constantly, testing the footing before each step.

Sometimes Lawrence fell to his knees. Then Louise had to lift him up, force him to continue.

Even the strongest, most tenacious climbers sometimes have to give up. When there is nothing left inside, when someone is completely exhausted both in body and spirit, giving up becomes the only sensible thing to do. Louise soon began to give up. She felt herself letting go, slowly accepting her certain fate. She was much less afraid of death than she had always thought she would be: to die under these conditions, on a mountain like Changamal, was nothing to be ashamed of. No — it was an honorable, respectable end. And it would come quickly, almost painlessly.

Now she thought of her parents. But that was an unhappy idea: to imagine how they would feel when they learned that she was gone, that she had disappeared. They had already lost one son, Rifi, in the mountains. Her mother might not recover from a second loss of this kind; and her father, despite all his years of experience in the mountains, despite his great climber's heart, would be utterly devastated. It was clear to her in these final minutes what a strong bond they had, her father and she: he had never felt anything but pride in her, and she had wanted nothing in her life but to make him more proud, to learn from him and try to be like him. Even now — even as she felt death quickly approaching — she was happy about that, satisfied with the choices she had made in her life.

She wasn't afraid of her own death, but she hated the pain it would cause to the others, to her family and friends. However, there was nothing she could do about that now. No, she had to let go. She had to leave her family to its own fate, let the people she loved go on suffering, hurting, living. That was what it meant to die — that there was no way to reach them anymore, nothing more to do for anybody. She had to accept this.

When her older brother Rifi had died, she had thought for a long while that eventually he might come back. The finality of his death hadn't made any sense to her; for years, she dreamed often that he wasn't really dead, that he had only fallen into a great crevasse, one of the deadly caverns of blue ice, and been trapped in there. But if he wasn't really dead, if he was only trapped, that meant there was something that they could do for him — some way to find him, to bring him back. This dream of hers, that her brother was still alive, only waiting to be rescued, had made things much harder for her; she had suffered with this idea for several years.

When she was about sixteen, she had had another dream. Her brother Rifi had appeared to her again: he was still lost, still in the cavern of blue ice, but he had grown more comfortable there. The cavern no longer looked so terrible, either — it was full of light. As she wandered through it, looking for Rifi, she saw how enormous and beautiful it actually was, with high, arching walls that gleamed like blue diamonds. Then she found her brother. And she saw that he wasn't afraid anymore — on the contrary, he felt protected here; he had achieved a kind of peace within the icy walls.

"Lawrence . . . Lawrence!" Louise called out in the storm.

Stumbling forward, she had come to the very edge of a crevasse. There was a dark opening in the snow; if she had taken another step, she would have broken through the fragile surface and fallen.

Lawrence came up behind her. He was very unsteady on his feet, weaving and staggering with each blast of the freezing wind.

"Lawrence — I'm going down. Into the crevasse. It's our only chance. We have to get out of this storm, or we'll be dead in minutes. Lawrence, you have to hold me on the rope — can you do it?"

"Louise . . . you can't go down there. You can't climb down into a crevasse. It's madness. . . ."

But Louise had an idea — a desperate, possibly suicidal idea. If Rifi, in her dream, had found protection within those icy walls, then she might, too. She arranged the belay, made Lawrence as secure as possible, several yards back from the opening, and then began walking forward again. She could feel the surface settling under her feet. Suddenly, it gave way beneath her, and she fell a short distance, then swung back against the wall of the crevasse, held by the rope. She was underground now, in complete darkness, dangling above the abyss. She kicked her crampons into the wall. Then, using her ice ax, she began climbing downward. She could see absolutely nothing below her, just the vast, terrifying darkness and emptiness.

The cavern was horribly cold. The air was like the air in a deep freeze, with a watery smell of ancient, unmelting ice. But there was no wind here, no punishing showers of ice and snow. And it was very quiet. The silence was almost perfect, a blissful peace after the howling storm above. She climbed down a little farther, and when her boots found a ledge to stand on, she said a silent prayer of thanks. Still unable to see anything, she felt the ledge with her hands and feet, and after deciding that it was just large enough, she signaled Lawrence by tugging on the rope.

She could hear him above her — she still couldn't see him, but by the sound of his crampons on the ice she knew where he was. "Straight down, Lawrence," she called up. "Only about ten yards down. I've found a ledge for us to stand on. We'll be all right here, Lawrence."

"All right. I'm coming, Louise. . . ."

Suddenly the rope went slack. An instant later, he fell on her from above, crashed against her. Both of them almost slid off the little ledge; all that saved them was Lawrence's ice ax, which happened to jam in the wall. Louise held on to Lawrence, then carefully pulled both of them back from the edge. Then, for several minutes, they simply lay there, on top of each other; they were too weak to move, almost too frightened to breathe.

Twenty-Nine

"Louise, I'm getting warmer. I can tell because I have pains now in my hands and feet."

"That means the blood's rushing back. That's good, Lawrence. Very good."

"I don't think I can stand it, Louise . . . it hurts too much. It's horrible. . . ."

They were jammed inside a single bag, a bivouac sack. Louise had carried the bag all during their climb, in anticipation of just such an emergency, and now it was saving their lives. The closeness of their bodies inside the bag kept them moderately warm. First Lawrence had rubbed Louise's hands and feet to restore circulation; and now Louise was returning the favor.

"Louise, did we actually get to the top?"

"Yes, I think so."

"I can hardly remember. It seems like years and years ago . . . I've been out of my head, I guess. I'm sorry."

"That's all right, Lawrence. It's just the altitude."

"And the lack of food; and the lack of water. But I'm feeling better now, more clearheaded. How deep is this snow cave, anyway? Or is it really a crevasse?"

"Oh, it's a crevasse, all right. I remember looking down into it this morning. It's one of those caverns that seem to go on forever, into the very center of the earth."

"And will we be able to climb back out of it tomorrow?"

"I don't know. But — why not?"

The cold soon penetrated the thin insulation of their bivouac sack. They were protected from the storm above, but the cold of the crevasse was like nothing they had ever felt before: it was only a matter of time before they succumbed to it. When Louise lay on the left side of her body, the cold penetrated and numbed her left shoulder, hip, and leg. Then she had to roll over painfully onto her right side. Meanwhile Lawrence, who was locked in a close embrace with her, also had to roll over.

"Louise, I let go of the rope. I let it fall down the crevasse. I'm so sorry."

"It doesn't matter, Lawrence. We'll get out of here anyhow. We'll think of something."

"Louise — why didn't you write back to me? Why didn't you ever answer any of my letters?"

It took Louise a long time to understand what he was talking about. Then she remembered: his letters, the way she had felt about them, all her pain and disappointment. . . . All that seemed to have happened ages ago, to someone else. Someone much younger, someone foolish and pathetic.

"Lawrence, what's the point?" she asked. "Why bother about that now? I've put it out of my mind. It doesn't matter to me anymore — not at all."

"Doesn't matter? Is that what you say? But it matters to me, Louise — it matters a great deal. You see . . . I changed my whole life. I did everything I could think of, everything to persuade you. When I wrote to you that I was leaving Canada, that I was giving up my medical career there . . . I heard nothing. Not one word."

After a moment, Louise answered, "But . . . did you say that you were leaving Canada? How could that be? I don't understand, Lawrence."

"Yes — two years ago now. Just after I left Marian. I wrote you about that, too — about how I returned to her in Paris, then accompanied her back to Canada, but that was the end. I owed her that much — after all, her family had been very kind to me. But I knew, after you and I climbed the Devil's Slide together, that I could never marry her. That I could never be happy with anyone else. You see, it was you I wanted, Louise. . . ."

As if to escape from the bitter cold, Louise rolled quickly onto her other side. But it was Lawrence whom she really wanted to escape from — from his words, from the confusion that they caused inside of her. Unfortunately, her attempts to escape came to nothing. The two of them were still tangled up inside the sack, and when she rolled one way, Lawrence did too.

"Yes — I left Canada for good," he continued. "I wrote you all about that. It was in my last letter . . . but you never wrote back. I guess I understand. You had never made me any promises, and you never said how you felt toward me. But somehow, I always thought that you and I would . . . well, that someday we —"

After a pause, Louise said quietly, "I never read your last letter, Lawrence. I put it away, unread. I'm so sorry. It was too painful . . . I just couldn't take it."

"Too . . . painful? Is that what you said? You never even read it?"

"No. You see — I missed you so terribly. Each time I got one of your letters, it made me feel that much worse. It made me miss you even more. You never said that you were going to leave Marian . . . you never mentioned anything about coming to Europe to live, or wanting to be with me."

"I didn't write about that," Lawrence explained, "because it wasn't all arranged. I couldn't say anything until I knew it would work out. But — did you really say that you missed me? That you missed me terribly?"

Louise made no answer. It was so dark in the crevasse, in the middle of the night, that Lawrence couldn't see her face, which was only inches away; but somehow, he knew that she was looking back at him, smiling. Since his arms were already around her, there was no way to pull her any closer. But even so, he tightened his grip, and then, searching for her lips in the dark, he clumsily kissed her on the side of her mouth.

Morning never really came. There was no dawn — no slow warming of the air, no gradual return of light to the sky. Down in the crevasse, no part of the sky was visible; even the hole on the surface, through which they had climbed last night, had been snowed over.

Louise had never fallen asleep. She was too cold for that; her hands and feet had gone numb again. She felt a deep, final exhaustion in her mind and body, as if her blood had actually stopped flowing through her veins. But she knew that she had to get up — they both had to start moving, or they would stay on this ledge into eternity.

There was a dim, eerie light in the crevasse — just enough to see by. Lawrence looked bad. His lips were blue with cold, and his nose and cheeks were raw from frostbite. His whole face looked much less healthy than before, much thinner: probably, he had lost twenty pounds in the last twenty-four hours. When he opened his eyes and gazed at Louise, he, too, seemed upset; and then it occurred to her that she probably looked just as bad as he did.

Without a word, they slid out of the bivouac sack. Louise, for no good reason, peered over the side of the ledge, down the sheer wall of the crevasse. It seemed to go on forever: if they had rolled off the ledge last night, they would have fallen hundreds and hundreds of feet, down into the deepest, blackest darkness she had ever seen in her life. Staring into this abyss, she felt dizzy and sick to her stomach — she had to force herself not to look, not to think about it anymore.

"I'll climb first," she said quickly.

"No — I won't let you go," he answered, just as quickly. "I'm the one who lost the rope for us, so I should be the one to get us out of here. I want you to watch as I climb. If the ice breaks and I fall, then you'll know where you shouldn't go."

"Lawrence, I'm a better ice climber. We both know that. Don't be ridiculous."

But Lawrence had already begun. He kicked his crampons into the wall, swung upward with his ice ax, and began to climb.

He seemed tired, even at the beginning. His movements were sluggish, and he grunted with each blow of the ax. But slowly he rose above her. Soon he was halfway to the top of the crevasse, where a roof of fresh snow blocked the opening onto the glacier. This was the greatest danger that they would face: where the wall of ice ended, they would have to dig and force their way through the snow. Without a rope for protection, and with uncertain footing in the surface ice, they would run a risk of falling back in.

"Louise, I can't do it!" he called out suddenly. "I'm finished!"

"Hold on! Hold on, Lawrence. Hang on your ice ax and try to rest. I'm coming up. . . ."

Louise had no plan — she only knew that she had to reach him, keep him from falling into the crevasse. Below them was nothing but darkness, the endless emptiness; with whatever strength that remained to her, she would save Lawrence from that. In a few minutes, she had climbed almost up to his position. He was barely hanging on, with his ice ax embedded in the wall and only one of his crampons firmly planted. To support him while she climbed above him, Louise drove their last ice piton into the wall, then tied the sling they had used yesterday to the piton, before attaching it to Lawrence's belt. Just as she did so, he let go of his ice ax; he fell heavily against her, almost knocking her off the wall. But she grabbed him around the waist, he grabbed her, and a moment later, she had kicked her crampons into the ice.

"Louise — don't let go of me! Hold on!"

"I am holding. . . . Lawrence, use your ice ax! Take some weight off that piton! If it doesn't hold, we're both finished."

Lawrence was afraid to let go of her. Not for his own safety — for hers. But he had to get his ice ax back (it was still embedded in the wall, three feet above his head). Still holding Louise with one arm, he reached carefully above him, groped for the handle of the ax, and finally took hold of it. Gradually he shifted more and more weight onto the ax, thus relieving the downward pressure on the piton.

"I've . . . got it, Louise. I think I'll be all right now."

Driving her own ax into the wall, she stepped away from him. She was completely exhausted — she had climbed too fast, forgetting how little energy she had left. And she still had to climb farther — then, to break through the roof of snow. She suddenly knew that there was no hope for them anymore; they had come this close, within yards of victory, but they were finished. She could probably climb the last little distance on the wall, but she would never have the strength to break through the surface snow.

"Louise — what is it? What's the matter?"

"It's . . . nothing, Lawrence. I'm just tired. I don't feel too well . . . I seem to have run out of energy."

"Take a rest then. Here, hold on to me again. I won't let you fall."

"No, I'll be all right. . . ."

They had come so far — they had done so much. It seemed a cruel trick of fate that they had survived the storm, that they had found shelter in a crevasse, after climbing the entire mountain, and now, just because they were a little too tired, they were going to have to die. It didn't seem fair. And their luck had been so good up to this point: everything had gone in their favor, every disaster had passed them by at the last instant. Why hadn't they been allowed to die on the headwall — or on the summit ridge? Why had she stumbled onto the crevasse last night, just as they were about to freeze to death out in the storm? What was the point of all this "luck," after all? It would have been better to die last night, out in the open.

"Louise — what's wrong? You're crying. . . ."

"It's . . . it's just that — I'm angry. I just can't do any more. I'm trying, but I just can't seem to . . ."

Louise pulled her ice ax out of the wall. Then — she slammed it in again, two feet higher up. She brought one foot, then the other, up onto the wall, kicking against it with her crampons. Soon she had climbed two yards above Lawrence's position. Then — four yards above. In fifteen minutes, she was at the very top of the ice wall. But here the ice gave way to mixed snow and ice. Her crampons no longer bit into the wall, and she had to kick out small steps to stand on. The snow and ice soon turned into pure, powdery snow, which no longer held the form of her steps. At the same time, she reached the surface layer of snow, the roof that overhung the crevasse.

She could feel her feet give way under her. She tried to swim upward, to push through to the top, but each time she grabbed an armful of snow, it came loose against her chest. She began to slip back. She could tell that she was about to fall — and she could also feel the abyss beneath her, attracting her, hungrily drawing her down. With one final thrust of her arm, she tried to drive through to the top. Then she began to fall, but at the same moment, something took hold of her, something held her tightly from above.

Thirty

That same morning — May 14, 1960 — Jean-François Maronnette and Anshak Rana, the two other members of the summit team, had set out from Camp 5. Maronnette was still not completely recovered from his intestinal illness. He felt weak and light-headed, but he knew very well that Louise and Lawrence, who had not returned from yesterday's summit push, were either dead or in a dangerous situation; they might need his help, and he was determined to do all he could to find them.

The weather was mostly clear, after a severe storm the night before. Anshak Rana led the way across the first snowfield. As Maronnette walked behind Rana, he caught a glimpse of the great headwall just below the summit. This was probably where the two climbers had met their end — the headwall reminded Maronnette of the top of the north face of the Eiger, one of the most dangerous climbs in the Alps. To climb the Eiger was one thing, but to climb its equivalent at an altitude of more than twenty-seven thousand feet was unthinkable. He admired the courage of his lost teammates, but at the same time, he wondered at the daring (or foolhardiness) that had led them to think that they might succeed.

At the end of the snowfield, Anshak Rana climbed onto a small glacier. The storm of the night before had deposited more than two feet of fresh powder, and many crevasses were completely hidden. At this point, Maronnette took over the lead from Rana, and he proceeded with great caution. If the other climbers had been turned back by the headwall, they might very well have retreated across this glacier. If they had fallen into a crevasse, there was nothing to do for them — their bodies would almost certainly never be found.

At 9:00 A.M., Maronnette and Rana reached the base of the headwall. They had seen no signs of an accident while crossing the glacier. Maronnette was exhausted; he sat down in the snow with his head between his knees, panting like a tired dog. To climb the headwall was out of the question now — he knew he would never make it, he would die up there. Once again, he had a strong intuition that his teammates had lost their lives here, that they had pushed on despite the impossible challenge. He tried to explain his idea to Rana, but the Sherpa guide, who spoke almost no French, could only shake his head and smile.

Maronnette had a strong need to lie down — to fall asleep in the snow. He felt confused, his head seemed to be full of cotton, but this was almost a pleasant, comfortable feeling — he only wished that Rana would stop bothering him, grabbing him by the arm and urging him to get to his feet. Rana was trying to say something now: his words were all mixed together, a hopeless garble of French, English, and Nepali. Finally, he gave up talking and simply set out walking — and Maronnette, who was still tied to him on the rope, had to follow.

They walked for a while along the base of the headwall. Then Rana pointed up: fifty yards above, where a narrow crack split the rock, something metallic was visible. Even at this distance Maronnette recognized it as a piece of climbing hardware, probably a piton. Then he saw a few other pieces of metal, all of them attached to the same area along the crack. It occurred to him that Louise and Lawrence had belayed from this place; or, having failed in their attempt to climb the wall, had rappelled back down from here.

But if they had rappelled down, there ought to be some sign of where they landed. Suddenly excited, Maronnette searched along the base of the headwall, and in a few minutes, he found a spot where the old snow had been trampled. (The snow that had fallen the night before had covered the trampled spot, but the flattening of the old snow was still visible.) Leading away from this place was a faint, snowy trail — it headed back down the glacier.

Eighty yards back, where the trail suddenly disappeared, Maronnette spotted something else. Someone had established a belay anchor on a broken pillar of ice; a length of climbing rope, still attached to the belay, headed off from the pillar to the right. Maronnette grabbed hold of this piece of rope and pulled. It came forward easily — the end of the rope was frayed, as if it had been cut or broken. At this moment, Maronnette lost all hope for his friends. It was finally clear to him what had happened.

"How terrible," he said, "how horribly sad." He tried to explain to Anshak Rana. The Sherpa guide, despite his lack of French, must have understood.

"They got this far," Maronnette said, "but the storm was brutal. Knowing that they were about to die, they took a last, desperate chance: over there, where the surface of the snow looks sunken, that's a crevasse. It's a snowed-over opening. They must have tied on to this pillar, then tried to lower themselves into the crevasse. They were looking for protection from the storm, but . . . then the rope broke."

Anshak Rana nodded his head. Yes, all of this was obvious to him; he had understood it even before Maronnette said a word. But though he agreed with Maronnette's theory, he wasn't yet completely without hope himself. He tied his own rope to the belay on the pillar, then began walking cautiously forward. When he came near the sunken area (the roof of the crevasse), he lay down full length in the snow. As he crawled forward from here, the snow under his body began to settle, and he prepared himself for a sudden drop. But just as the snow roof began to give way (Maronnette was holding him from behind on the rope), an arm came thrusting desperately up through the powder. With unthinking speed, Rana grabbed hold of this arm — he grabbed hold of Louise, who, with the last bit of her strength, had managed to break through to the surface.

Epilogue

The climb of Changamal by the northwest face has never been repeated. In 1964, a party of German climbers reached the base of the headwall, but bad weather forced them back. Then, in 1972, two Polish climbers reached the top of the headwall — they were last seen walking along the windy ridge, headed for the summit. But they never returned to camp, and their bodies have never been found.

Lawrence Darnley, who had to be brought out of the crevasse with ropes, lost three toes to frostbite. He never again attempted a first ascent in the Himalayas. However, to this day he climbs actively in Europe and North America. For many years he practiced medicine in the town of Montier; now he divides his time between Montier, which remains a small, beautiful village, and the much larger city of Grenoble.

Louise DeMaistre also lives in Grenoble now. Her many other climbing exploits have been described in films and television documentaries. For the last twenty years, she has served as director of her own climbing school, which is headquartered in Grenoble. Louise and Lawrence have three children. The oldest, a son, never enjoyed climbing very much, and the second, also a son, climbs only occasionally, on an amateur level. (Both sons are grown now and live in Paris.)

Louise's third child, a daughter, resembles her father rather than her mother. She has Lawrence's brick-red hair, beautiful warm smile, and eyes the color of new leaves. When this girl, whose name is Martine, was about eleven years old, she went climbing for the first time (she had always been afraid of heights before, and she was seriously overweight). She had a good time, to her own surprise, and she asked her mother to take her climbing again soon. But Louise was leaving the country at just that time; she had to go to South America, where, with the other members of an international expedition, she reached the summits of Aconcagua, Cerro Torre, and other famous peaks.

While Louise was traveling with this expedition, Martine went to live with her grandparents, in Montier. Jules DeMaistre was then more than eighty years old. He moved very slowly, "like an old tortoise" (as his wife said to tease him), but he still loved to climb, he still loved being in the mountains. He began to take his granddaughter out on short, daily rock climbs. By the time Louise had returned from South America, the stiff old man and the plump, pretty young girl were almost inseparable. Louise was astonished by how much her daughter had grown.

"Yes, she eats well here," said Jules DeMaistre. "And the regular exercise seems to suit her. I think she'll end up a tall one, like you, but with a stronger body."

"And have you made a regular climber out of her?" Louise asked. "Is that what you've done, Father?"

"Well — that's not for me to say. Speak to her yourself, Louise. But I have to tell you something interesting. Just last Thursday, we went out to climb Henry's Hat together. When we were about halfway up the face, it started to rain, and then the rain suddenly turned to hail. I set up a rappel, so we could get back to the bottom. But Martine stopped me. She said: 'Grandfather, I don't want to go back down yet. I want to go on, to the very top.'

"And I said to her: 'But do you really think you can do that, Martine? And in this freezing rain?'

"And she said, 'Well, I don't know about that. I don't know if I can really make it. But something makes me want to try. Yes — I know that I have to try.' "

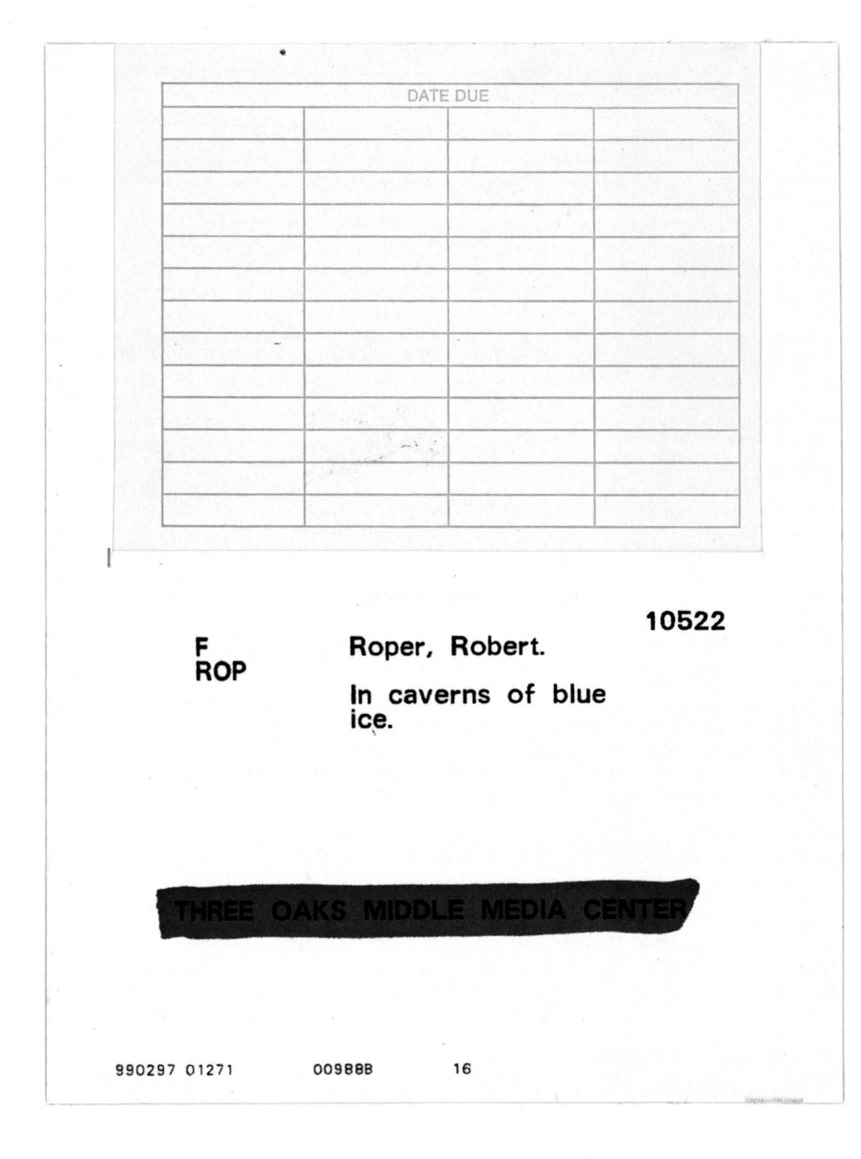
DATE DUE